Books by Joseph J. Kozma

Until We Meet, poems
Mathematics in Color, poems
Long Distance Murder, mystery novel
Killer Plants, a poisonous plant guide
Of Song, of Life, chap book
Solitary Bee, chap book

1945

Joseph J. Kozma

Burning Daylight

Copyright © 2011 Joseph J. Kozma. All rights reserved.

Published by Burning Daylight an imprint of
Pearn and Associates, Inc.
1600 Edora Court Suite D
Fort Collins, Colorado 80525
For information about publishing please
contact happypoet@hotmail.com.

Cover design by Terry Orin, Orin Design & Graphics.
Thank you to Betty Hamman, David Whiteing, and
Spirit Lowrie for proofreading *1945*.

This novel is a work of fiction based on the lives
of many nameless individuals
who one time or another had similar experiences as
the characters of this book.
The narrative follows an actual time sequence
without reference to a calendar date.

Library of Congress Control Number: 2011933627

Kozma, Joseph, J.
1945 by Joseph J. Kozma. First edition.
ISBN 978-0-9841683-9-2 paperback

PRINTED IN THE UNITED STATES OF AMERICA
Canada, United Kingdom, Europe, and Australia

First edition

Dedicated to all who find the way.

Contents

Chapter One . 1

Chapter Two . 24

Chapter Three . 37

Chapter Four . 49

Chapter Five . 58

Chapter Six . 70

Chapter Seven . 91

Chapter Eight . 113

About the Author . 133

Chapter One

The spring of 1945 was not at all unusual. It looked the world over, like always, it felt like always and smelled like always. Only what happened in the spring of 1945 was different.

The spring, as a rule, works the beginning of many things. Rivers start among snow crystals, millions of little threads enlarge and swell. Finally, they boast a name and make a mark on the map. Many loves start in the spring and carved names appear on the tree trunks just as the sap emerges, driving up to the sky. Ants like the fresh carvings that smell like life. Nations rise against their oppressors and people break the chains of slavery.

Weather beaten walls take up new shades of colors and brushes run across their faces. Nests are built, repaired and robbed. Bird feathers turn lustrous and strange sounds penetrate the silence when the sun rinses the countless acres below and when the moon mops up the warmth of the day.

Doctor János Nándor was walking on a narrow sidewalk, heading west. He had not been in Szombathely too long. He, like thousands, was a refugee from the eastern and southern part of Hungary. He was thinking of the power of spring. The great balmy months of March that he remembered contrasted with what he saw around him and what he felt this time. The great festivities of the 15th of March, the exuberance of the celebration of the Hungarian revolution of 1848 was now like a distant mirage, not approachable, suspended, if not for ever, at least temporarily.

***

It was three o'clock in the afternoon. The street was dirty, littered with broken glass, plaster and bricks. There was no traffic. He heard noises and weird sounds generated by saws and the pounding of innumerable hammers. He saw people on the roofs, in the windows and at the doors, hammering and repairing what was damaged only a few hours earlier by extensive bombings. He could still smell the unmistakable smell of the explosions, a combination of dust and heat producing a lingering irritant to the senses.

He finished working on his house. He boarded up some of his broken windows, secured his front door and was heading to his job at the Health Department.

The shock of the severe bombing that destroyed a third of the city suspended in him all connections with the outside world for a while. Now as he was on his way to work he found his surrounding to be a new experience. He felt like he was entering a strange, new world with a strange, new breed of people who paid no attention to him. He saw the creation of hundreds or thousands of limited worlds located in every house and every street corner. The universe ceased to exist or at least became very limited. It was replaced by the hope for survival.

He lived in a house that would have been vacant had he not been quartered in there by the authorities. When he arrived in Szombathely he looked up the Health Department. It was located in a small one story building, obviously not designed for accommodating any kind of office. He found the director in a room in the basement. There was much emptiness in that basement room, hardly any furniture, just a large table, few bookcases and boxes and boxes.

He was greeted by Doctor Szántó, a friendly stocky man with a mustache and a full head of hair, almost too black. He sat in a comfortable easy chair. It did not match the table. There were more chairs in the room, none of them matching. They did the job in a nonconformist way forced upon them by the war.

Doctor Szántó stood up and greeted Doctor Nándor warmly. It was a greeting that almost felt like good-bye to János. In war when the clock is ticking and one smells the acrid vapors of gunpowder, actions and motives change and loose their original character. There is fear and suspicion in everything. For just a fraction of a second János felt something like that. Soon he felt comfortable.

"Call me Sándor," he said, obviously tried to make János comfortable Sándor was his first name. He asked him about his trip to Szombathely.

"Do you have any place to stay, do you know anybody?" He asked. The answer was "No."

"Let's take care of that now," he looked at János smiling and made a phone call.

"The police will be here instantly and will take you to a nice house where you can live while you are working for the Health Department."

"Am I?" János asked.

"Of course," Doctor Szántó said, have a good rest and come by tomorrow early afternoon. I'll give you the details."

A policeman arrived. Soon he had a roof over his head.

***

The owners of the house sought shelter and safety in the country, the policeman informed him.

Next day, around noon, the air raid found him in the living room. When the wailing of the sirens entered his ear canals and caused a resonance in his ear drums his electrified nerves gave him a command to seek shelter across the yard in the basement of a three story building. It looked like a sturdy stone edifice that has seen better times.

He was late. As he ran across the hall he heard a grinding noise as if enormous cars were trying to start. A thud followed that rocked the house. Some plaster fell from the wall. The thuds became numerous and came closer and closer. Soon everything rumbled, shivered and convulsed. Then the rumbling went under ground followed by bursts into the sky. A steady, grinding noise served as a background to the roar, scream and laugh of the airplanes. After the first explosions, in a second of delusion, he thought that he was safe. He heard that you never hear the bomb that kills you. As long as he heard the explosions he was in no danger. He reached a small, glass covered platform that led to the back yard and tossed himself on the floor.

He was in the path of what was called a "carpet." Precision flying super bombers laid down the carpet that consisted of five ton or larger bombs chained together to provide good coverage. At least that was what everybody feared. If you were in a carpet you had very little chance for survival.

The planes came, wave after wave. He was able to see some of them dip before releasing their bombs. He felt air pressure against his body, against his lungs as the bombs exploded. They were close, He even felt the heat generated.

The entire attack lasted around twenty minutes. He lived through it. His house suffered minor damage. Two houses to the left houses were flattened except for the chimneys. They stood in defiance, pointing to the sky. "They did it," they accused.

The chimneys stood up under the bombing much better than other structures. Even when a house was turned into dust and everything looked like a pile of dirt, the chimney stood proud and accusing. He saw some photographs of Budapest after a similar bombing raid. In the rubble many chimneys stood solid like giant tomb stones.

As he walked he felt renewed. He felt reborn. He was dead for twenty minutes. He was exactly like dead with no chance of generating life or even to defend what heated him through his twenty five years. He had no contact with the world. His senses turned to the inside. He heard his heart pleading with his ears. Toward the end he was in a complete state of hibernation not being aware of his existence or of the existence of other things. He was dead. Then he noticed the silence. Then he noticed his own breathing, then his heart and his weakness, in that order. After that he felt calm, much alive and ambitious.

***

In March of nineteen forty-five the western portion of Hungary was still in German hands. This small area was Transdanubia, basically the territory enclosed by the river Danube on the north and on the east, the river Drava on the south and the Austrian, now German, border on the east. The government moved from Budapest to Sopron, very close to the western border. Some of the Russian forces crossed the Danube and were close to Szombathely. There was a fluctuation of the front-line. At times one could hear the canons greeting each other and conversing. This happened mostly at night when exhausted nerves longed for relief and when dreams could not decide between the past and the present. The future was darker than the night.

Many thoughts and emotions floated around, many ideas and no deeds. There were no flag bearers; there were no loud voices, only whispers. The Nyilas Party, the Hungarian Nazi Party, was not in evidence. It was rumored that while the government was moved from Budapest to Sopron, Szálasi, the Party leader and head of the government did not stop there. He went on to Germany. Nobody really thought that Germany would win the war. There was a faint hope that the English forces operating in the south somehow could reach Hungary and keep the Russians out. This hope was alive before the Russians ever entered Hungary. Now at this late, when the end was just a short time in the future, it was washed away by sighs and the wind carrying the smell of gunpowder.

Nerves were exhausted, people who for years believed in Goebbels' promises of secret weapons with super destructive power, now, closed their ears and listened to their own senses.

There was a rumor that large units of Russian troops died in a mysterious way. Some of the dead soldiers were standing, leaning against trees without visible injury. Gas warfare was suspected, test of the secret weapon was suspected, guesses and imaginations changed the eternal pattern of spring.

Eyes could not see colors. The houses were in ruins, smoky and gray like fall fog. The ears heard only thuds of explosions and rumbles from the sky more persistent than thunder and more deadly than lightning. The fingers did not touch warm, freshly baked bread for the ovens were cold. The air tasted like sand, sharp and cutting, causing the gums to pucker. This all spelled one thing, Germany was dead.

In a last minute struggle, before retreating into Austria, the government issued a decree that made it mandatory to deliver all bicycles to Party headquarters within forty eight hours. There was a severe shortage of gasoline, and the bicycles were to give speed and transportation to the infantry. The deadline passed about two weeks earlier. Now as the doctor walked in the littered street, he saw a large number of bicycles scattered in the ruins. Attics, basements, yards were exposed by the bombing, unwrapping bicycles that should have been delivered to the Party building to be confiscated. These bicycles were testimonials to the faith of the people and the outlook of the war.

***

As he walked more to the west and closer to the square, he passed by an unremarkable house. It was unremarkable in every respect except that the sidewalk was swept clean in front of it. A German officer stood in the door putting on his gloves quite leisurely. His uniform was clean and seemed freshly ironed. It was the kind of uniform that the Germans called *tadellos*. He stood there a little while then started to walk with strong, loud steps. He acted self assured. He was well fed. The house that he left behind was gray with cracked stucco wall just like the other houses. The Gestapo took up quarters there a few months earlier. Since then the sidewalk was swept everyday.

The doctor and others in the neighborhood knew that it was better not to be aware of that building. He kept his eyes focused ahead and narrowed his peripheral vision until he saw only the square in the distance. He walked by this building daily. An internal warning told him not to look. He controlled his eyes well, but he could not inactivate his eardrums. Moans, groans and screams caused him to hurry. An unconscious urge to get away entered his muscles. His brain registered only vaguely.

When he was a little distance from the building, his mental functions including objectivity returned. Life has a meaning for everyone, he thought. Some people never realize it and never think of it. Others think of it so much that they have no time to live it. Eternal youth is suspended somewhere in between moving unceasingly. Motives influence these motions that are considered good or bad depending on the judging parties. Some of these motives were opposed by the rulers. They had to be eliminated. The Gestapo basement served that purpose.

***

A young German soldier, looked around nineteen, walked across the north side of the square with full battle equipment. He was dirty and staggered some. Behind him, the sun made the dust swirl. It was cold, but his uniform was unbuttoned. His neck and a part of his chest were exposed. Clotted blood was covering his right temple. His eyes were alert.

People stopped to look at him. There was neither sympathy nor hatred in their gaze as they followed him with restless eyes.

At this phase of the war hatred almost disappeared. If nothing else, it was modified. Hatred is a luxury and a fad. It was triggered at the beginning of the war and became fierce in 1940. Hatred was the specialty of politicians and those who were able to avoid the draft. Their lips frothed with hate, danced on the airwaves, they wanted to make hate a way of life. They snuggled up to the Germans because they hated the communists, the Russians.

The men in the trenches felt different. They knew that only survival could and should be the goal and hatred was something that could cloud your brain like a strong drink. The fighting man relied on his reflexes. He relied on them to act for him. How and when they acted was crucial.

Those who did not fight sometimes philosophized. "Everybody will lose in this war," they said, "even the winners." "Everybody is in the same boat now," they told themselves. Hatred was replaced by "philosophy."

The soldier did not pay attention to the people.

He was about six foot tall and blond. He was one of those youths on whose shoulders rested the future of Germany. He was called for active duty right after Christmas when his school was closed and all of the seniors were inducted. He had a short course in battle conditions and was sent to the front. Around the end of January his unit was stationed on the west bank of the Danube, 30 miles south of Budapest.

Further south the Red Army crossed the Danube and started to push west. An almost continuous see-saw battle went on for a long time, perhaps a month. The Russian army was pushed back several times as far as Szigetvár, the site of the legendry self sacrificing attack of Zrinyi against the Turks hundreds of years earlier.

He fought during February. His unit was in constant motion. Casualties were high. Göbbels used two magic words to convince the troops and the population that the hardship and sacrifice were worth it. The enemy would be annihilated. That would happen in the basin with boundaries of the Danube on the east, the river Dráva on the south and the Lake Balaton on the north. The Russians were crossing the Danube at Mohács. That point would be eliminated then strong panzer units would move in from the west and annihilate the Russians.

In February, the German armored units rolled into this area and pushed the Russians as far back as Pécs. There was complete lack of reinforcements and the Russians were not cut off in Mohács. At that time the German strategy had the earmarks of grand delusion. There was catastrophic shortage of gasoline and their air power was virtually absent.

The German forces regrouped several times and attempted the annihilation. It happened whenever fuel supplies arrived. They reached the Danube several times but they could not hold their positions. The lack of fuel, rain and mud and blood stopped the annihilation.

Further south the Germans put on a show by reoccupying the part of Croatia between the Dráva and the Száva rivers. The German propaganda started to blurt about the secret weapons again. Total German victory was again riding on the winds. The winds stopped soon, but not soon enough for the dead.

The events of the south exerted a temporary influence on the Russian troop movements. For a short time it looked as if the Russians could be isolated in the "basin." Moscow saw it too and the Red Army began to retreat to the east and take up positions behind the sheltering width of the Danube. At the western part of this Russian held triangle a few small towns were evacuated by the Russians. The news of this burst into the tired winter air with the freshness of spring. The German supported government came out of hiding and jubilantly prepared to move an administrative force into this area. The Nyilas Party had the job to send experts and other manpower to take care of the job.

Members of the Party who took refuge in western Hungary were asked by press notices to offer their services for the liberated territories.

Dark suits were dusted, cleaned and ironed and the Party armbands of double headed cross arrows in a white circle surrounded by the Hungarian colors of red, white and green started to appear on the sleeves of the dark suits of those who offered their services.

A group of these volunteers was gathering on one of the street corners watching a German propaganda movie displayed in one of the show windows.

The German soldier looked at them for a moment, slowed just a little as if he wanted to stop. He was slightly off balance. It looked as if his knees would buckle. Then, he kept going. They did not notice him. He was alone, not followed by other soldiers. It was a strange sight even at a time when events rarely seen were an everyday occurrence. He carried his gun in his left hand and his cap in the right. He went westward but he did not follow the streets. He found paths between the ruins, he crossed the yard and entered doorframes that lost their brick support and now connected two sections of the same, heavy air.

As he reached the outskirts of the city, his eyes seemed to focus far ahead into the infinite distance of the hazy, blue sky. His thoughts were ahead of him. They rode on the cool, swirling wind toward the west; toward his home. He did not notice the houses. They were fewer now. These houses did not show the scars of the war. His steps became heavy. His knees were closer to the ground, bent but his head remained upright. At a street corner he stopped for a moment, and then a strong north wind mowed him down. He collapsed.

Within a few minutes a green-gray German ambulance stopped. The soldier opened his eyes. His face asked, "how did you get here so fast? Who notified you?"

He closed his eyes and his lips turned gray and thin. He did not notice the warmth and comfort of the heated ambulance as it picked up speed. A medic entered his name in a ledger, Heinrich Wolfgang, Gottlieb, Berlin.

There was a rumor in March; a sweet rumor for many, that Budapest was still in German hands. The city with thousand years of proud history still resisted, symbolizing Hungarian freedom for thousands had died over the centuries.

Being occupied by the Germans was the lesser evil; it was closer to freedom. The Government was silent. There was no solid information. Rumors and, at times, legitimate news have mysterious ways of getting around. This was the case now. Some people claiming to have left the burning city just hours earlier gave accounts of fierce, heroic fighting against terrific odds. The city changed hands several times, so they said, but for weeks nobody really knew who held the capital city.

Photographs of indescribable destruction were circulating, showing damage of the parliament building and other public structures. Some other pictures showed graves of soldiers buried in public parks and back yards. Some of the tombs were marked with names burned into wooden crosses but most of the time only heaps of dirt represented testimonials to civilization. These pictures, at times, brought comfort to the relatives who found refuge in the west because they knew that even in the hours of desperate killing the dead had the respect of the living. The rumors insisted that Budapest was alive and fighting. The rumors were surrounded by mystery. How did food and materiel to fight with reach the city? It was known that most of the territory between the Lake Balaton and the Danube was in Russian hands. There had to be an artery still pulsating and keeping Budapest alive.

At that time Slovakia, which was created in 1939, after the German occupation of Czechoslovakia, was firmly in German hands. The popular belief was that supplies for Budapest came through Slovakia and transported across the Danube. The theory while far fetched had some feasibility to it.

The doctor reached the square. Few people were standing on the corner reading the "Signal" magazine. "Signal" was published in Germany in several languages including Hungarian. By standards of the day, it was very well done. Of course it was designed to spread the good word about Germany and Hitler. A large pile of the magazines was leaning against a building and a young boy was announcing the latest edition in a shrill voice. He had one copy in his hand. The pages made a swooshy noise attracting more attention as he waved them high above his head. The doctor reached in his pocket automatically and bought a copy.

The date was September 1944, obviously not the latest issue. This was a significant fact. In war dates and facts have a way of becoming questionable, to say the least. Last September's issue in March of 1945 hardly could be the latest, as the paper boy announced. Was the magazine not published anymore? He opened it at random. Crisp drawings met his eyes. Human hearts were depicted as they behaved under the strain of a *Stuka* attack. Some of the pictures showed how the blood was displaced within the heart, with one chamber essentially empty. Looking at these pictures, suddenly, made him realize, what he should have realized before, that there were no *Stukas*. There was no German air power anymore. Months earlier, when he left his home town, he watched the planes landing and being loaded and taking off, soon heard the thud that, he thought, came when a tank was hit. The front was that close. When they still had them, the Germans used a *Stuka* against a tank approach. He remembered the skies of 1940 swarming with the German Air Force. He also remembered when Göring promised to supply the Sixth Army with food and ammunition in Stalingrad "for any length of time." It was said that because of that promise Hitler withdrew the land forces and left the Sixth Army behind. Now the Sixth Army was gone and so was the air force.

A large contingency of Russian prisoners of war was ushered by German guards in a westerly direction. They hurried in formation, strangely empty handed.

They did not keep pace. Their uniforms were a mixture of Hungarian, German and Russian. Their footwear consisted mostly of rags wrapped around their feet and tucked under their pants. These prisoners were members of the victorious army. In ironic contrast, the German soldiers who guarded the prisoners wore good uniforms, dirty but not torn. This was the first time the doctor saw Russian soldiers. He was never in the army. He was a medical student in the early phases of the war and was allowed to continue his studies. More than soldiers, skills and devotion were needed, particularly doctors. The wounded were shipped home to receive care. He just received his diploma when his home town was evacuated. With just his clothes on and his diploma in his hand he started west. He did not say good-bye to anyone. The sky was red in the east and the cannons roared ceaselessly. Soon his footsteps were covered by exploding bombs, blood and torn bodies.

The people on the corner discussed the "Signal" pictures. A fat, bald man with glasses and protruding belly explained in an oily sounding voice why he did not believe that the pictures of the heart were an accurate description of the physiologic situation during dive bombing. The people listened. Nobody asked about his credentials. His lower lip was hanging as well as his lower eye lid. Phlegm was building in the corner of his mouth. Another man, likewise with a big stomach in striped black trousers complete with gray grass stains, nodded frequently. Others interrupted and stimulated the discussion.

For some reason, the doctor remembered this group of people for several years. Years after the war when he was watching *Lady and the Tramp* in New York City, the dogs singing behind bars, reminded him of the small crowd on the corner in Szombathely in 1945.

In just one hour the "Signals" were sold. Glossy, multicolored publications were rare in those days. The Germans provided that rarity. The men were gone now but the corner was not empty. Another crowd gathered, men, women and children. They were looking skyward and pointed with agitated fingers. It was four in the afternoon. The sky started to turn gray and started to lose its blue. It assumed a milky color that made the sky brighter than the earth. Some people experienced an eerie feeling. They watched a shiny object that was whiter than the white looking sky. "It must be a balloon," somebody ventured. "It is only a star," somebody answered. "Maybe the secret weapon," the small boy added in a timid voice.

They stood there in agitated groups of three, four and even six. They all looked up to the sky and assumed that the other groups were watching the same thing. They were all well dressed. Some women had fur coats. The night was still cold. Spring cautiously oozed around the streets and provided some warmth, not enough to get rid of warm clothing. The men were mostly in dark suits, some wore vests. These were mostly refugees from the eastern part of Hungary, from cities like Szeged and Szolnok or from the south like Pécs and Szigetvár. As they packed to start their journey to the west, they picked their very best clothes. Now that was all they had.

A crowd has a magnetic quality. It has magic powers that expand and force others to join, convinced or just curious. The crowd grew larger and larger. The eyes were trained to the sky where a bright object like an early star vibrated and looked suspended. For seconds it disappeared into the depth of the universe then reappeared. Its size never changed. It appeared regularly everyday at about the same time causing more and more daily excitement.

As the night broadened and the stars became brave and started to show their faces the crowds disappeared.

All kinds of explanations surfaced. Those who were dominated by their religious beliefs regarded it as a heavenly sign for a gloomy future. The rebirth of the world was in the making. This was a warning for remorse and to prepare to die, and to make space for a newer, cleaner healthier world.

In 1940 many people would have accepted without questioning the notion that German brains, German planning and German purpose placed it up there. Now only a few thought it to be some secret of the Germans. The majority regarded it as a celestial phenomenon.

There was no basis for any of the explanations. Opinions were based entirely on feelings. They relied on them in the practice of everyday life. They were tools for survival. In the bitter spring of 1945 most people followed their intuitions. Thinking was a pleasure of the past that was left with their houses, and belongings. Thinking required facts, solid facts and consistent patterns. The population did not have facts. They had no markers that could be used to measure their lives.

Hitler's words were flying around without wings and fell to the ground with each Allied success. The refugee government was in self-isolation with very little contact with the people.

Szálasi, the leader whose power, as he claimed, was given to him by Horthy mocked Hitler in many ways. These days he was not available even to the members of his cabinet. He holed up in a basement somewhere near the Austrian border. He wrote his memoirs; he was not to be disturbed. To him the chaotic conditions were unreal. Nobody was to disturb the man who was in the process of creating important documents for the future. His cabinet members were scattered; some were in Germany. Some people thought that Szálasi was too. A few optimists moved about in the small area that was still in German hands, made speeches and spread words that nobody believed. Rumors of atrocities of the advancing troops in the east added to the generally desperate feeling. Endless darkness fell upon the population in which life seemed to be suspended.

Celestial phenomena often intensify negative feelings and create a restless state of mind. It was a great relief when night dropped on the city and the gleaming object disappeared and gave the sky to the stars.

***

It was almost five in the afternoon when the doctor arrived at the Department of Health. His working hours were eight to twelve and two to five. Today's routine was interrupted by the bombing. Before leaving he boarded up his broken window and picked up the door keys scattered on the floor. Every key to an inside door, even for cabinet doors was blown to the floor by the pressure released by the bombs. He did not attempt to do any cleaning. The plaster was badly cracked and some of it fell forming thick layers. The dust settled some by the time he left.

Dr. Szántó, his boss, knew why he was late. There was no damage around the makeshift Health Department. Most of the bombing hit the railroad station and the surrounding area. The station now was leveled; tracks were twisted, many pointed to the sky.

The Health Department squatted in a small house. It was white washed inside and out. The rooms were small. Some of the offices were located in the basement. Dr. Szántó operated this institution single handedly and according to no particular schedule or purpose. Drugs were not available. Biologicals were nearly forgotten. Occasionally a

German shipment of Typhoid vaccine would arrive. The general population never would know about it because only friends and relatives would be vaccinated. The small supply lasted just a few days.

"How are you János?" Dr. Szántó greeted him as he entered. "Is your house damaged? You can come to our house."

"No, I was lucky, only a few broken windows and dust. Inside, the house looks like a battlefield. I hope this was all for today."

At this time really nobody could imagine that the destruction would ever end. The nerves were strained to exhaustion but giving up was harder than turning the pages of history that as yet were to be written.

Dr. Szántó greeted János in his small office across an over dimensional, heavy desk. It was clear that this piece of furniture did not come with the house. It was probably rescued from a government office, perhaps even from Budapest. Still, the doors and the windows were small, not able to accommodate the huge desk. It got in there anyway.

"I want to tell you about a job that I have been planning for some time. I just did not have the man power. I don't want to lose any more time. I will put you on it tomorrow." He looked around, and then he continued. "You know we have no medicines. If an epidemic of any kind would break out we would have no protection and no means to fight it." He stood up and opened the door of a large cabinet with yawningly empty shelves. He started to pace. He could only take a few steps in the small room, and then he had to turn around. He paced a while then he said, "If we can prevent an epidemic we can go on until we can produce again. We have a huge problem. People are dying because of lack of medicine. You know that insulin is completely unavailable. I don't worry about insulin, he added. It is mostly for the Jews."

"I haven't seen digitalis either. My father-in-law has a heart condition. He has not had digitalis since Christmas. Right now he does not need it badly. He lost a lot a weight and feels better." János nodded.

"These things don't worry me too much. But, people are dying from pneumonia because we have no sulpha, or we are losing children with diphtheria because we do not have a drop of antiserum, makes me feel as I could choke." He gripped his throat.

"Therefore I am going to comb the city for carriers of disease and I want you to get started early tomorrow morning. I'll get you as much help as you need. Here is the plan."

He took a city map opened it up and spread it on the table.

He looked like a general planning the next troop movements. The doctor looked at him and recalled that in the history books you have a difficult time finding a date that is not connected with the name of a general.

"We will divide the city into sectors. Szombathely is divided naturally by its streets and the river. We will take advantage of that." He pointed to them on the map. "We will take each of these segments and check every house. We will cover every office. I am sure there is somebody at home in every house nowadays. Virtually everybody has refugees living with them. This refugee problem is getting out of hand. Now look at this." The map looked like a jigsaw puzzle. The segments were outlined in various colors. There must have been 30 segments, it seemed.

"I want you to start here." He pointed to the northwest corner of the map. "A policeman will go with you just in case. Some people are jittery nowadays. Take your time and do a good job."

"What am I to do?" János asked.

"Oh, I am sorry. I almost forgot the most important thing. You will check the houses and people, and I repeat people, for lice and other bugs. Check their coats, collars, beds, belts whatever you like."

János wanted to say something but Dr. Szántó cut him off.

"Yes, I almost forgot. It seems that I forget too many things. Here are your credentials."

It was card that said, "This is to certify that Dr. János Nándor is employed by the Department of Health for the purpose of uncovering lice in the city of Szombathely. Long live Szálasi! And it was signed Dr. Sándor Szántó.

This certificate was written on a typewriter with green ribbon. Green was the "official" color of the Nyilas Party. The members wore green shirts in imitation of the German National Socialist Party whose members wore the "brown shirts" the "Long live Szálasi" was an imitation of the Heil Hitler on German documents.

Around 1:00 AM, when the cold of the night was at its peak, several deep rumbling sounds and unmistakable shots could be heard. They sounded far away toward the east. There was quiet for a while. At 2:00 AM the sounds returned as if one heard some delayed echoes. After that there was quiet. Not even a Rata flew over the city. The morning cold had difficulty opening the eyes of the people who lost sleep listening through the night.

The doctor too, woke up in the middle of the night. He could not go back to sleep. He lay holding his breath, listening to the darkness. Toward morning he dozed off. When he awakened, he vaguely remembered the echoing noises of the distant shots. He was tired but he started on time. He was joined by a policeman at a prearranged place.

He knocked on the doors and rang the doorbells according to his schedule. His face was honest and sympathetic. The population's response was excellent and he was received politely by almost everyone. A few people demanded soap and complained bitterly about the various shortages. A few people were timid, obviously afraid. A large majority approved the Health Department's program as a step in the right direction. At times when death by raw force dominates, it is easy to forget the natural disasters such as epidemics. No war, no systematic eradication of a segment of the population can compete with nature's killers, infectious germs.

The doctor entered the houses, examined the beds by lifting up covers and by looking into the folds of bedding and into the cracks of wooden bed boards. He looked at the people's personal clothing, turned up their collars, loosened their belts, and examined their hair and arm pits. That did not take very long at all and caused very little personal embarrassment.

János was surprised how well his approach was accepted. Everything went smoothly until around 3:00 PM when an incident occurred. He remembered it for a long time. He entered the large living room of an elegant house. The furniture was of excellent quality and the room was arranged with good taste. There were expensive looking pictures on the walls. There were needlepoint's in gold frames. The occupants were dressed as if 1945 never existed.

A sweet smell was lingering in the room, the sweet smell of pleasure and satisfaction. Here was the sweet smell of freshly brewed tea. Tea was scarce in those days. A large bowl of cookies, like a source of inexhaustible energy sat proudly on the piano. An exquisitely decorated plate with small, typically Hungarian sandwiches looked inviting. It seemed that he had walked in on a party.

The room looked completely out of place and of time. The houses that were just one block away were flattened. There was debris and dust everywhere. Here, there was old time elegance, art on the walls and abundant food. The doctor learned that, indeed, this was a small afternoon Party. The doctor was not aware of parties in this late phase of the war. Food was an item surrounded by secrecy. Housewives would stop cooking and hide the ingredients if the doorbell rang. Nobody admitted to having reserves. Meager were the times and more meager times were expected. Fear of starvation was as genuine as the fear of loneliness. Many persons had more than their shares in both of these categories.

Five ladies were sitting in comfortable chairs. There were no men. He introduced himself, explained what his mission was and asked them for their cooperation. There were no objections. While making conversation, he proceeded to examine their clothing. The lady of the house was very charming and explained that the party would start as soon as her husband returned home from work.

It seemed that the ladies enjoyed the situation. They giggled and made some remarks but were not insulting and they were not political. János felt a relief. He was tired of the almost ceaseless rhetoric he was exposed to on his way to the west.

He apologized for the inconvenience and was ready to leave when the head of the household arrived. He was a middle aged man, around fifty. He was tall with grayish hair arranged in large waves. Now that the hair was disturbed by the wind it looked like two triangles pasted to his head above his ears. He wore a black, heavy overcoat with a velvet collar and a silky white scarf. He held his brimmed ray hat in his left hand.

He looked around questioningly as he entered. His wife, a little timidly, explained to him what Dr. Nándor was doing. She actually introduced the doctor to her husband.

"You are next Ernö," somebody called giggling, and two women grabbed him and pushed him in front of the doctor. As they stood face to face János explained the purpose of his mission. The man asked a few questions and the whole thing seemed to roll on like on schedule. It was not unpleasant at all, the doctor thought. He asked the man to turn around. He examined his hair, especially the long temple hair. He turned up his shirt collar and he lifted the lapel of his jacket. He felt a slight dizziness when he saw a louse crawling out from under a lint deposit. He almost felt guilty.

What does one do in a situation like this? He tried to contemplate in a hurry. How does one call attention to a louse? Is it best to be triumphant and make some indignant semi official comments about the health of the population and of the nation, or is it best to be apologetic for the unfortunate discovery and offer the services of the Health Department? While he was thinking, which seemed like eternity, the louse crawled into plain view followed by petrified expressions of the elegant ladies. It is remarkable how much contrast a single louse can create.

All of a sudden there was a real question. What was real, silver, china, fine furniture, tea and tasty cookies . . . that was the real world until the discovery of the louse. What kind of role can a miserable parasite play in the world of glitter? There was a surprise on everybody's face reflecting assessment of realities. With a louse the war intruded, it could not be ignored. It had nothing to do with the condition or sanitation of the home. It came from the office, probably a small isolated incidence.

As he did not get anywhere with his hesitation the doctor suddenly grabbed the louse and said, "Here." The man turned around and asked, "What?"

"A louse."

"A louse?"

"Yes."

"You put it there, you god damn communist." The man shouted. "You are going around trying to hurt decent people." Just what do you think I am? Get out of here. Get out."

The man was indignant, agitated and unreasonable. The doctor thought that he believed in what he said. If it were so, it was a good sign because he was not a fake. His accusations were absurd. His wife rushed to him while the others just retracted into themselves. She tried to calm him the best she could. In spite of that he became more and more agitated and shook his arms and hands wildly. He looked grotesque.

The doctor tried to explain but he got nowhere. He listened quietly and absorbed the accusation. They were as much out of line as the louse was in this elegant home. He was still holding the parasite. He tried to decide what to do with it. Finally, he put it on the window sill and crushed it with his thumb nail. Two ladies wrinkled their noses in disgust. The others found it quite funny. Finally, they all giggled. The man kept on cursing. Dr. Nándor left.

The next day took him into a less impressive neighborhood. He visited a gypsy village at the edge of the city. A certain air of mystery surrounded the gypsies. There were all kinds of stories about them.

Earlier in his life János had contact with gypsies when he was on vacation in the summer at his grandparents. Gypsies over the years managed to be different from the rest of the population. Some of their characteristics created stories like digging up buried carcasses of farm animals and eating them. Old neglected houses, castles in wild forests, mighty rocks, lights in desolate marshes, places where bloody revolutions had taken place carry a halo that sometimes turn into curse. The gypsies through hundreds of years of Hungary's history preserved a type of isolation that destined them to live in their communities, usually on the outskirts of cities and villages.

Hungarians weren't exactly sure how to treat gypsies and how to accept them. The doctor never heard any or read any authoritative discussion about the origin of the gypsies. He only knew what he heard when friends and neighbors had some discussion about them. He heard that there were two different types of gypsies. Both types inhabited not only Hungary, but the countries of the Balkans, Russia, Romania, Bulgaria and others. Both spoke Hungarian with a strange accent. One group spoke a language that was similar to Romanian, that in addition to their Hungarian. This group excelled in work and was honest. They did basket weaving, wood carving, repair work and more. One could see them in the city going door to door selling wooden spoons. "*Fa kalány*" they would announce instead of the correct "*Fa kanál*," meaning wooden spoon. They remained fiercely independent and few had some kind of employment. Many of them were excellent musicians. They were sought after as entertainers. Hungarian Gypsy music became world famous. Liszt, Bartók, Kodály borrowed from the music of the gypsies. Gypsy violins were excellent interpreters of Hungarian folk music. These gypsies conducted a stationary life style and their children attended public schools

Another group of the gypsies were thought to be Egyptian in origin. Their language had nothing to do with Hungarian or Romanian. They did not settle down in a particular area. They were constantly on the move; they were thought to be nomads. They claimed to be horse traders. Somehow they always managed to have a pocket full of money. They frequently got into trouble with the law.

There was a gypsy village belonging to the first group of gypsies just outside Szombathely. It was located approximately one mile to the south on a narrow dirt road. Roads are like dogs, they have no prejudice and serve their masters faithfully even when abused or neglected. The road showed bad neglect. The settlement consisted of some fifteen houses with walls made of clay. They were white washed showing their smiling white teeth. The houses were clean on the outside. On the inside they were simple. The furniture was barely adequate on clean clay floor. That kind of floor needed to be watered frequently to keep it from getting dusty. One of the doctor's aunts had a floor like that. In the country this type of floor was not unusual in those days. There was no floor covering. The roofs consisted of straw. They looked like shocks of hair over square faces. They were combed straight down and created a large overhang with irregular edges. Two houses were different. The roofs were covered with typical spade shaped-shingles. They looked like the backs of over dimensional red snappers.

The gypsies either were clean all of the time or were informed in advance about the doctor's arrival. They were meticulously clean. Their clothing was likewise. Their shirts were freshly washed and starched.

Several small children were running around in the cold weather wearing clean ironed shirts. They were barefooted and their naked buttocks were red from the cold. The gypsies were pleasant and polite. They were obviously adaptable. That quality must have been their protector over the centuries.

***

One afternoon the air was sweet and warm. Some birds acted foolishly on the roofs, and the sky revolted against the winter. It was good to feel the sun which trickled down timidly. The knotty wind changed directions frequently bringing waves of the warmth of the south. It appeared as if the blades of grass assumed a slight glow rendering them crunchy under the pressure of walking feet. The doctor was working near the city square.

He left rows and rows of residential houses behind. He was now in a warehouse section. There were several businesses located in this part of town. Police escort was no longer needed because the procedure was well accepted and serious incidents did not occur. Occasionally a woman would exhibit a well orchestrated emotional plea demanding soap, food, hot water and the like. She would blame the government for the lack of everything.

At times some unsaintly terms would be used. In such cases, the doctor sympathized with the complainers. That calmed the nerves. He entered a court yard that was surrounded by a large U-shaped two story house boasting a balcony protected by impressive iron work. There were apartments on the second floor. The first floor served as a warehouse of agricultural equipment. This was a good breeding ground for rats and cats. Nearly a dozen cats lay in the sun, well fed and lazy.

The stairs were steep, quite unsafe due to a lack of rails. That some time in the past there were rails, could be seen in the regularly protruding rusty iron in the concrete. He climbed up and knocked on the first door. He felt the warmth of the sun on his shoulders as it smiled from behind. Few rays skipped by his shoulders and found their way into the room. It was dark inside; there were no windows. He had to wait a few seconds to get accustomed to the darkness. He kept the door slightly open and waited while his eyes were able to register a strange gray haze in the otherwise empty room. It was a large room with wood floor and no furniture. Some of the floor boards were missing. Much plaster was missing from the walls visible in the meager light coming through the door. Debris was piled high in the corners.

Extraordinary things have strange effects on people. The doctor's reaction to an unusual event consisted of throbbing in the throat and repeated swallowing. This time his throat was virtually paralyzed because he noticed two things almost simultaneously. They made an extraordinary and lasting impression.

The one thing was a person, a human being, for a few seconds without any gender identity but soon becoming feminine as she sat on the floor in the corner. Pieces of potato sacks covered her. There were no seams and the pieces fell loosely from her shoulders. She kept her legs crossed. Her knees were large and her ankles slim. Her legs looked like a pair of exclamation marks. Her hair was dark, long, uncombed and dirty. There was a suggestion of a part in the middle. Her right hand rose slightly and something incomprehensible left her lips. One or two teeth could be detected in the upper jaw as she opened her mouth. The rest were either gone or were black in the darkness.

When she lifted her hand, the light became a little more intensive in the room. He became aware of the second thing that caused the human figure to vanish from his conscious mind. He was not sure what he saw. The uncertainty made him dizzy. There seemed to be a veil floating about three feet above the floor.

It was undulating rapidly like the wings of a large slow flying bird or like a black flag on a coffin in a storm during a funeral procession. He had not seen anything like this before; he was unable to categorize it. It was ghostly. In a few seconds that felt like eternity, his senses sharpened. His trained mind quickly tried to be analytical particularly because he heard a slight noise. The noise was like a silk breeze, blowing over velvet leaves, and rolling the satin grass. There was a mass of fluctuating density in front of him with a veil on top moving endlessly and exploding frequently.

The noise was caused by the bottom of this mass pounding against the dirty floor like fog turning to droplets and dropping on a tin roof. The vision and sound were impressions first, but his brain, almost paralyzed, recovered quickly and solved an unexpected real life puzzle. Silently, he stepped back from the door and closed it. He was on the balcony now. Just then he noticed that he was short of breath; he must have held his breath. He opened his mouth and nostrils and inhaled deeply. He knew what he saw. This unbelielievble airy mass of airy density was caused by innumerable fleas jumping off the floor frightened by the sunshine and the squeaking of the door.

The following night was interrupted by another bombing. This time the bombs were scattered seemingly without an attack plan; they were dropped all over the city. The next morning the house with the fleas was replaced by a crater and piles and piles of debris.

Wisdom even when it is extraordinary and brilliant, when it is applied to the past, is called hindsight. Hindsight seldom finds past glory. It invariably points to something that should not have been done and should not be repeated under the same circumstances. Such hindsight was plaguing many people these days that spent many nights summarizing and analyzing the past and trying to make deductions for the future.

Their thoughts were never really transformed into actions, not even into words because the birth of such words was mortal sin in the eyes of the rulers. By this time many people thought that some kind of neutrality of Hungary should have been arranged, although nobody believed that it would have been respected by the Axis Powers. An alliance with the western powers, while it was sympathetically viewed by the population, could never have been possible.

Building-up ties with Stalin wasn't desired by anyone. What else was there left? It was only ruins and defeat. Ruins and defeat could not have been avoided, but maybe the national honor could have been saved. France was free, so was Poland. Unfortunately, freedom did not mean the same thing all over the world. The shades of freedom were as many as the colors of the rainbow and just as intangible.

Air raids were numerous now. The sirens howled two or three times every night. The alarms lasted anywhere from fifteen minutes to two hours. Nerves were drying up very rapidly and impulses found faulty connections. The sleepless nights were visible in the population that moved about in the daytime like in a trance, almost immune to further insults.

The American Air Force dominated the sky now and flew missions day and night. The Russians flew mostly at night using outdated aircraft.

The evenings were warmer now. Mild winds brushed the heads of tulips as they looked eagerly on the south side of the houses with full expectation to live. Snow drops grouped their white heads together watching the ground carefully for signs of warm steam. In the midst of all the destruction, killing and death at least one evening was beautiful. Nature provided a break. The night looked romantic and quiet. The warm air with the smell of millions of past springs created a mood sensed only at night. "Never before and never again," was the mood of the night.

The doctor was tired and went to bed early. It was his habit to review the events of the day, trying to remember as many details as possible. That way he kept his memory in good working order. He had that habit since his high school days. It served him well during his years in medical school. Tonight he cut his contemplation short and dropped into a deep sleep.

It was late in the night when he was awakened by a howling noise followed by the sound of an explosion. His head was buzzing and he felt slightly dizzy, disoriented was a better description. He remained in bed for a few seconds listening, trying to put everything in perspective. Then he jumped out of bed and tried to find orientation by the weak light seeping through the cracks of the pulled window shade. He did not dare turn on the light. He hesitated only for a fraction of a second before he realized what the terrifying howling was and found himself on the way to the basement.

The noise became louder and closer. Now one could hear the distinguished purring of an airplane or two.

"The old coffee grinder" he murmured "with a new gimmick." The Russian RATAS were called coffee grinders in Hungary. A few months later when he was in Germany, he was told that the Germans called them sewing machines.

Once he realized what was going on, his nerves calmed. Russian warplanes were flying over dropping their bombs at random. They were mostly ineffective. If they hit a roof, the shingles broke, that was all. Some people did not take shelter. János did; he went to the basement, just in case.

Before returning upstairs, he looked out of the basement window. The sky was burning in a bright glow. The street was bright almost like in the daylight. A huge Stalin candle was hovering over the city generating many guesses. Some people thought that the Russians were just outside the city and the light served them with added visibility. People in fear and panic left their houses and congregated in the streets looking up to the sky and down along the houses. The German guard stood motionless in front of the Gestapo building under the cover of a doorway arch.

The howl of the bombs was terrifying. They sounded like thousands of bloodhounds tracking and searching. That noise stopped when the bombs exploded. The Russians used sirens on their bombs to increase panic. This was the first time such bombs were used in Szombathely.

As he looked across the street he saw his neighbors standing in pajamas and overcoats. They acted restlessly and gesticulated wildly. Their backs were humped from sleeping spine and agitated mind.

Short, sharp blows of whistling hit his ears and commas of lightning bounced off the street. A machine gun growled ceaselessly. Tracer bullets criss crossed madly. The planes were combing the streets with their machine guns. He watched his neighbors disappear into their houses. Soon the ordeal ended, and he collapsed into a deep sleep that made him part of the universe.

Chapter Two

"Good morning. Do you remember me?"

"Sorry, I don't believe . . . ."

"Well, you were so preoccupied and may I say embarrassed that you did not see the people. That is all right. In doing a job one must be absorbed in following a goal even if it is only a louse."

He raised his eyebrows slightly, and then looked at her long and questioningly.

"Well, I see you don't remember. I am the daughter of the gentleman under whose collar you found that louse. You should have heard him after you left."

He remembered the incident but did not remember her. There were other women in the room. The whole thing was very embarrassing. She was right.

She was neatly dressed in a brown knit suit and wore brown shoes. He thought that she was quite attractive. At this point a little ceremony took place though considering the circumstances there was very little need for it. Following Hungarian customs he formally introduced himself. He learned that her name was Maria Magyar. She asked him to call her Marika. Of course she was to call him János.

This happened at the general hospital, a huge collection of monster structures scattered among monumental trees on spacious grounds. The doctor was sent there by Dr. Szántó to inquire about the supply of sulfa drugs and other medications that may be available at the hospital. Dr. Szántó had a secret and grandiose idea that involved the inventory of sulfa, namely Prontosil and other drugs such as Salvarsan. He gave János a list.

Marika was a student. Her parent's home town was Debrecen, which they left in the summer of 1944. War interrupted her studies and forced her to prove herself in a number of different ways. She turned out to be quite good in odd jobs and had many of them. As they moved west she found various little jobs wherever they stayed for a while. When the Red Army captured Debrecen the Magyars moved to Budapest. There Marika worked as a typist at the Army Headquarters. In the course of her work she stored everything she heard and observed. While assessing the situation she convinced her parents not to stay in the capital city but to move closer to the Austrian border. It was because of her insistence that the family got out of Budapest long before it was completely encircled by the Red Army.

In Szombathely she became a secretary at the general hospital. She eventually wound up in the pharmacy. She was to keep an inventory for the use of drugs and supplies. Because there was very little to keep track of her days were spent in reading and thinking.

Financially she was independent. Her father was one of those well situated people who preferred the solidity of gold and diamonds over paper. He invested his money into tangibles. He inherited large holdings of farmland. He had excellent timing. He lived in the city but he managed to be in the country at harvest time. His mansion was south east of Debrecen. He was one of those few feudal landlords who did not feel that machinery was an intruder. He spent large amounts of money and imported German agricultural equipment. The dividends were great. His wealth increased rapidly, and in due time, he was able to purchase the title of Baron. That way he could enjoy a few advantages including the friendship of the members of Parliament, and later in the final years of the Horthy regime, the sympathetic feeling of several cabinet members.

He had no sons. Marika was his only child. It was always his ambition to become a statesman. He, like many people had a vision. He visualized himself followed by his daughter in state service. But, that was before the war. The realities were different now. Even now, he thought that good connections had an undisputed edge over qualifications. Even wealth and family connections were not enough. A woman in politics sounded radical but he considered it possible.

He was an ardent Nationalist. He stood with all of his emotional might, of which he had abundance, for the revision of Hungary's borders which was "violated" by the treaty of Versailles (in a room called Trianon, hence the treaty of Trianon) after the First World War. "The Pesti Hirlap," the largest daily newspaper, popularized a picture of the crucifix with the broken shape of Hungary replacing Christ. This was surrounded by a halo and by the words, "Nem, Nem, Soha," (No, No, Never). An over dimensional rendition of the picture decorated his study. It adorned the east wall opposite to a west window. Baron Magyar managed to invite friends to his study just when the sun was departing into the endless depths of the universe behind the western horizon and it lent the picture an eerie halo for a while. The broken body of Hungary nailed to the cross lay in the bloody-red rays of the sun for a few minutes. At such time, with a gesture that was remembered by his friends and guests, the Baron pointed to the west and in a trembling voice said, "There is the source of our salvation."

The effect of such a statement was unique in that those who sympathized with the Germans thought that he meant Hitler. There were others who as early as 1936 the time of the Berlin Olympics looked toward England. So, Baron Magyar was popular with all political fractions except the communists whom he considered his mortal enemies. Since the communists did not have political status, it really did not matter.

Until the Anschluss of Austria, it looked like peace would prevail in Europe. It looked like it in spite of the Murder of Dollfuss and the Balillas of Mussolini. In 1938, when the German power reached the western border of Hungary and when the first Vienna award went in effect, giving part of Slovakia back to Hungary, Baron Magyar made very few statements. He still had his revisionist feelings. He kept his emotional balloons uninflected. He changed his attitude when the Horthy regime made a pact with Germany for the return of a portion of Transylvania.

In 1939 his daughter started to study political science at the University of Debrecen. She was the only girl in her class. It was more or less a sensation while it lasted. In spite of her father's insistence she switched to philosophy. She was very quick and very impatient. It was very hard for her to stay with her course and take some of the philosophical principles one by one starting with elementary concepts. It was hard for her to study the details and neglect the total picture. To her it looked like spending time to observe nails and bricks and not seeing the building at all.

She developed a system of her own that covered a great variety of subjects. She had views involving the state as well as the individual. She had a paralyzing quality of opinions and expression that made her controversial among the students but it made her loved as well. She aggravated her professors because of her advanced readings. She was bored with her classes. She quit after two years. She intended to finish someday. The hopes of Baron Magyar to make a politician of his daughter shattered. For the sake of simplicity Marika remained a philosophy student. She liked it much better if people thought that she was a student of philosophy.

She wasted no time and began bombarding Dr. Nándor with her most beloved slogans.

Philosophy has a special way of invading the convulsions of the human brain. It is unfortunate that without verbal expressions philosophy cannot exist. It is also unfortunate that verbal expressions frequently become the purpose of philosophy. It was, to a large extent, that way with Marika.

"What made you join this louse-searching crew? You are a doctor not a sanitarian," she said.

"I agree with the statement portion of what you said. Now, you want an answer to the question or was the question just an introduction?" He said.

"No, really, I want to know. My image of a doctor is . . . ." He interrupted her.

"Your image of a doctor is what you read in the books. The devoted image of complex, civilized creature that is incapable of thinking like a human who is like a robot, wears a white gown and wears a spotlight on his forehead that has grown to his head like the branch of a tree. Am I right?"

"You are sarcastic," she remarked.

"Yes."

"You might be right. There is something romantic and heroic connected with my image of a doctor. Yes, I read some books but I much rather think it is because of our old doctor at home. He was gentle, always smiling and eternally busy."

"That is nice," he said and laughed.

"What is funny?"

"Nothing," he paused, "I am sorry."

Marika suddenly raised her voice. "What do you mean my doctor's image is that of a man incapable of thinking humanly?"

They were still standing in the reception area of the pharmacy. János was in a hurry so he made no effort to answer. On the other hand he hated to interrupt the conversation. He actually liked to discus doctors in general and liked to listen to people as they spoke about doctors.

He was busy trying to take an accurate inventory. It was a difficult task because the supplies were not in a particular order. He counted injections, pills, syrups, suppositories, ointments and other less important items. Marika was helping, that made the work go faster.

During the few hours of work he noticed her more and more. She was well dressed. She was the right size, he thought. She was not plain, but if her eyes, lips, nose, her neck and shape were considered individually she presented a certain beauty. He could not understand how the cumulative effect of beauty could be less than the sum of the contributing parts.

He asked her if he could walk her home after work. She agreed.

As they walked she started the conversation. "You . . . well, the man with the louse. It was funny. My father raved for hours after you left."

"I am sorry. It is really unfortunate. One can pick up a louse anywhere nowadays. A coat rack, for instance."

"Never mind apologizing. An apology makes one automatically guilty."

"Or just polite," he remarked."

"If the apology is not sincere it can poison the subconscious."

"I am poisoned," he laughed.

It was fairly cold but not freezing. It was the kind of temperature to which any mood can adjust rather readily. János was amused by her talk and her obvious effort to be impressive.

"Being poisoned is curable. Being poisonous is contagious and permanent." She said.

"The world is curable, then."

"Is it poisoned?" She asked

János thought that she was playing with words.

"Yes," he said. "It has been poisoned, for some time, maybe not the world but certainly our part of it. Hardly any one of us realizes that we as individuals have been poisoned by the past thousands of years. I guess we should be proud. We live in a time when history is molded into a different but certainly not final shape. I regret only that it is being molded on our backs as our backs change their shape."

"Shapes really don't mean anything, what's underneath the crust is what counts." She said.

"And what is there?"

She looked as if she were thinking, then, almost giggling; she said "Nothing." We were so darnn nationalistically educated that I almost forget that nothing much is backing up my words any more."

All of a sudden she looked relaxed. It was quite dark now. The streetlights were not turned on. János felt a force that held her together. She was attractive at that point.

They said good night with the customary handshake and made no plans for another get together.

In the following days, János managed to see more of her. She looked more and more attractive. A mutual friendship developed. Gradually she got rid of her stern and more or less argumentative behavior and was cheerful and full of music.

She stopped playing with words. Her thoughts were truly deep, full of meaning. János admired her for her philosophy of life. It shocked him at times. He had trouble deciding whether what she said was theory or some hidden or even forbidden experience.

The noons started to get warmer now. The golden sunshine churned up imaginations and desires and it looked as if the tree branches started to bud and put life between the earth and the heaven.

During lunch hour the doctor and Marika walked among the huge trees that surrounded the hospital. The ground was warm on the surface but cold was escaping from the depths causing the ground to be moist and ruthless. Each time the air raid sirens sounded the work stopped. Patients and personnel took shelter in the trenches that were dug throughout the gardens among the trees.

The doctor was working at the hospital now. Everyday, for a few hours, he still visited homes as an employee of the Health Department.

There was a bunker built from dirt and logs. The doctor and Marika sat down on a dry log. The day was delightful; the sky was vibrating slightly and was noiseless. Innocent birds behaved like fools. Huge elm trees and oaks spread their branches protectively.

She was telling János how much Salvarsan was used lately. The hospital was just about out.

"In times like these venereal diseases naturally increase," he said.

"Naturally?"

"Yes, the moral values are torn down and the confusion creates an easy way to cover up. You know how prostitution is spreading nowadays and you see often enough that many Hungarian girls attach themselves to German soldiers knowing well that their usefulness will end soon."

"Perhaps you wanted to say, their use, but, in any event, I don't think that prostitution is really more prevalent now than in peace time. The difference is that now hiding and cover up are not necessary because, as you said there is apathy and general confusion. What you call prostitution is really free love turned into financial enterprise. The real prostitute is a social entity. These girls and women who run around with the Germans and with our own are not really prostitutes. Believe me, many just have a good time, enjoying it primarily and receive financial rewards as a side line."

She stopped, listened for approaching airplanes, then continued, "Women have a more pronounced capacity to transfer their biological characteristics into what some people call 'spiritual activity,' tea parties, cocktail parties, theater or just simple things like raising children or darning socks. The very fact of respectability may be enough to create a status quo of satisfaction resulting in little or no sexual desire. One would think that women who seemingly enjoy the blessings of a highly developed civilization could go wild and live in orgies like it is said of some ancient civilizations. The opposite is true. When civilization breaks down the biological takes over. The shimmering surface loses its faking power. This is what happens today. Destruction and dirt, elementary desires like hunger, thirst and the desire to sleep and survive bring out the desire to enjoy the only modality given to humans at birth. Many, of course, get caught in this sweeping grind and wind up here at the hospital. We are loaded with them. Why should we judge them, they just lost their games?"

"You would make a good defense counsel," he said.

"No defense, nobody is guilty."

He could not quite understand her. He could not conceive that she could possibly believe what she said. On the other hand, if she believed all this, then she almost had to have a reason, more or less justification. This thought made him uncomfortable. In a way he felt foolish. She really did not advocate anything she just stated facts or just explained some facts. What she said about the biological sounded to him not like a woman, but more like a man. Yes, he thought that could have been said by a man. It looked to him that the circumstances washed away the basic division of humans, making them just Homo sapiens. Only now they could hardly be called that.

In a sudden spurt of bravery, he lodged a question; he thought was leading, but not insulting.

"What does your philosophy do to you?"

She looked surprised and burst out laughing.

"I wonder if you think I am different."

He did not answer. They stood up and walked around under the huge trees whose dry skin started to pick up moisture. They kept close to the bunker and spent their time in discussion.

They had known each other a little while now. The thoughts of the other became more familiar and less novel as they expressed themselves to each other more and more freely. They became more relaxed and played games of reading each other's mind. János liked this intimacy. It was like enjoying freedom with nothing to hide. He related his inner most thoughts to her and seemingly she did the same. That created an element of happiness between them.

As he learned more about her spirit he became more attracted to her physically.

The all clear signal sounded. People crawled out of the trenches and many diaphragms relaxed, and drew in the fresh spring air thereby revitalizing the bodies, which grew numb in the crowded shelter. If there was a time in the twentieth century when safety was as sweet and nourishing as mother's milk, the time was now.

János stretched into the sun dotted air. It was a good feeling. He asked Marika to go with him to the movies later that evening.

The screen was gray and the theater was dusty. The cleaning crew, if there was one, apparently did not bother with the dust. The light beams of the projection lamp cut a sharp wedge into the dancing, bouncing dust particles. The movie was about two doctors. One was the hero, one was the villain. The hero was a crusader, devoted and highly ethical. He crusaded in the hospital and in political circles. He moved about almost perpetually doing good here, devoting himself there, and appealing to the sympathy of the spectators. His patients thought that he was a saint, followed him with enthusiasm.

His opponent was a less devoted doctor. At least that was implied on the screen. He got the girls, mostly the heavy ones. Weight reduction was his specialty. While the devoted doctor was nearly starving and was in financial jam, the other doctor prospered and got the girls. But toward the end everything turned out all right because the good doctor knocked him though the window and made him land on the side walk. After that the good doctor received an award. Nobody could see a reason for the award. Nevertheless everybody felt satisfied.

The newsreel was more interesting. For the first time, in several months a picture of Hitler was shown. After the assassination attempt in 1944, Hitler did not appear in newsreels in Hungary. He looked changed in March of 1945. His head was hanging and his upper back looked as if cracked. He wore gloves and his left arm seemed paralyzed. He was not the same Führer people hailed a few years ago. He was so unlike him that the movie goers thought that the picture was a fake and the person they saw was an impersonator. They were convinced that Hitler died in 1944 when the bomb exploded. Some believed that he was alive but they did not expect anything. He was like a washed up actor without applause.

***

Even though chaos and defeat were knocking on the door, political meetings were still frequent. Perhaps even more frequent than before. The Nyilas Party, now in power advocated vigilance and advised fighting to the very end. The Party was the government, army, welfare agency, court and police. More and more people in civilian clothes with armbands were carrying guns.

Work details of Party members and recruited civilians were digging trenches east of the city. They were erecting road blocks of large logs supported by stakes and braced by dirt. Only a few uniformed Hungarian men could be seen. The major portion of the remaining army moved to Germany to be reorganized and *ausgerüsted.*

The population only knew that the army was gone. Occasionally a few young men wearing the uniforms of the Hunyadi Brigade were heading eastward to the frontline that was not more than 30 miles away. The Hunyadi Brigade was an imitation of the German *SS*. The members were young men, mostly students who joined the brigade because of their revisionist education conferred upon them from birth. They had nothing to do with the *SS*. Their uniforms were similar. Instead the *SS* they had an H on the collar. They did not serve Hitler in spirit. They knew that Szálasi sold them out. At this point they were committed without a chance to turn around. They did not know for whom or for what they fought. They only knew against whom they fought.

The Rome-Berlin axis was almost forgotten. The glorious Hitler-Mussolini Treaty vanished from the memories of the people. Nobody really considered northern Italy to have had any contribution to Hitler's war. The front on the west as well on the east crumbled. Everybody knew that the proverbial "only a question of time," could mean a question of days. People were desperate. Suicides occurred frequently.

There was a Party meeting in a large house at the east end of Szombathely. The rooms were filled to capacity with Party members who wore dark suits. The walls were decorated with the crossed arrows, the symbol of the Hungarian National Socialist Party (Nyilas Party). A loud speaker system related the words and slogans to every room. The members sat at tables along the wall. Most of them did not see the speakers at all. The attention was focused on the loud speakers. The eyes were looking into an imaginary distance. Many of the faces expressed dreamy expectations that never materialized.

The meeting began with the song, "Ébredj Magyar az Ősi Föld Veszéjben." (Wake Up Hungarians. The Ancient Land is in Danger). Like so many things in those days, this song represented an imitation of the German custom of singing another song in addition to the National Anthem. The German song was Horst Wessel.

Nazi Hungary divested itself of all Hungarian originality. The land with one thousand years of culture, with legendary national pride, with peculiarities and values of its own was firmly established as one truly great nation. Under Szálasi Hungary became Germany's shadow imitating Hitler and the Germans. Szálasi, to imitate Hitler, wore a Hungarian private's uniform.

The program consisted of a seminar on bravery based on Hitler's *Mein Kampf.*

The speaker read the passage in German then in Hungarian translation. He elaborated on the subject of bravery in relation to man's ideals and came to the conclusion that ideals do not exist without bravery and vice versa. He rejected Platonic ideas. "Ideas exist only after humans establish an ideal for which they are willing to show great deeds of bravery." He said, "An ideal and bravery will give rise to the birth of an idea, which will perpetuate itself only as long as a human force exists behind it. Nations that have lost the force of bravery have lost their national ideals, and therefore, the idea of that particular nation ceases to exist, and the nation dies. It becomes absorbed by other masses of people. The loss of bravery is the greatest crime a human can commit, and must be punished by death."

His speech lasted about two hours. A discussion followed that consisted mostly by adding to the line of thought of the speaker. There were neither objections nor criticisms. The walls listened patiently behind the drapery of flags and emblems. The walls were very good, patient listeners.

Baron Magyar was at the meeting. He was not a Party member He was invited by a friend.

The Baron could not believe his ears. He thought that all he heard was absurdity. At a distance of not more than a few hours of walking the front was bulging, it was about to break and these people, in the shelter of that warm house spent the night discussing abstractions dreamed up by a maniac. He could not decide what he really heard, a political or philosophical extravaganza. Neither one had a place in these days of desperation. He has had enough of philosophy that his daughter forced upon his ears day after day. This meeting made him mad at her. He could have slapped her. As he was thinking about the events he got more and more mad at her. He could have killed her.

* * *

The doctor was bothered quite frequently by sore throats and enlarged tonsils. Though he worked in the hospital, he could not get anything more specific than Aspirin. Medicine was not available. The small inventory that he was able to record earlier was now gone. He felt feverish and achy. He took eight Aspirins a day without relief. He kept going to work first but finally, when his wrists and fingers turned red and swollen, he gave up and stayed at home. He knew he had borderline rheumatic fever. The bed became his companion and his best friend.

The house was cold. There was no wood or coal. The storage areas in the basement were empty. By now they had forgotten what they were created for. The fuel situation was poor; the food supply was just as bad. He had no bread, no potatoes, and no vegetables. The only nourishment he had on hand was a few pounds of smoked country ham that he was able to buy two weeks earlier. He stayed in bed for three days.

The bedroom was large, and originally it must have been tastefully furnished. Time and circumstances robbed the bedroom of its character. Now it looked more like a warehouse rather than a bedroom. Furniture was stored in every corner and the closets were inaccessible. Books were piled up near the bed. As the eye shifted from one corner to another the character of the room changed from warehouse to bedroom to den.

During the three days that the doctor spent in bed nursing his sore throat and aching joints, he had time to think and read. He read two books in two days, *Quo Vadis* and *Ben Hur*. He was greatly impressed by them and enjoyed them immensely. While in bed and reading, he dozed off frequently.

When he woke up he compared the two. He looked at their literary value and could not decide which one deserved to be number one in his mind. In a way they were different, in another way they were similar. He decided to read them again and compare them when the circumstances became more favorable.

Those three days had a great influence on his life. He was in complete solitude. Nobody knocked on the door and he had no outside connections. Occasionally he watched the people walking in the street and deducted from their expressions and their speed that the military situation was about the same. During the day he heard no cannon fire but the Ratas made a visit every night.

He had lots of time to think. He really did not concentrate on it. It was automatic. He became restless. On the second day of his solitude he became aware of the need for a decision concerning the future. There was a visible retreat. One could see fewer and fewer German soldiers. Only a few military transports moved in an easterly direction. Most of the traffic hurried to the west. The frontline moved westward.

New rumors started everyday. They appeared like migrating birds, fluttered around and disappeared as the distance swallowed them. The latest rumor concerned the south of the land, which was thought to be still in German hands.

The air was fairly warm and his windows were cracked. A burst of breeze would come from the west from time to time bringing with it fragments of Lillie Marlene. Riding on the wings of the western wind the song came from the square where a German loudspeaker poured it into the air continuously.

"*Da wollen wir uns wiieder sehen, for der Kaserne woll'n wir stehen, wie einst Lillie Marlene, wie einst Lillie Marlene.*"

Lillie Marlene was more than a song in those days. It was information, the only information available. As long the song was on the air, the station was in German hands. Radio Belgrade played it around the clock. The rumors were true the south was in German hands.

The song kept on beaming deep into the night. Fragments flew through the window like butterflies during the day and like bats when the night took over. "*We einst*," like sometime ago. Many things existed in memory only. Even yesterday became some time ago. The past can be comforting at time, but for the doctor it meant confusion and unreality.

He had to think clearly. His mind was boiling in a pot of the past, the present, probabilities and possibilities, just a mixture without solid and predominant content. Here he was clinging to a small corner of Hungarian soil. Soon the soil would be overrun and reorganized. Yes, it would remain Hungary, a different Hungary, to be sure. He wondered what difference that would make. Hungary had changed many times during the centuries.

What difference would one more change make? He recalled the passage. "Áldjon vagy verjen sors keze, it élned és halnod kell." (Be blessed or damned by the hands of fate, here you must live and die). He wondered what the fate of the individual would be under Russian occupation. The news that somehow found its way through the frontline was unimaginably bad; wholesale plunder and universal rape were reported. He knew that he would have to arrange for his own fate. Organized governmental actions no longer existed and society was falling apart. There was no recognizable similar desire of the masses. Everything became a slogan. Everybody was on his own. The doctor felt an enormous pressure of solitude descending upon him. There was a satisfaction in that, his future moves were genuinely his.

All of a sudden the question became simple. Without discussion, relying only upon a message from the universal consciousness of the world, he had to decide to stay, or move on to the west. To stay meant occupation and new order, to go west meant new order and a different kind of occupation. He decided to go. His goal was to go west and keep going until he would reach a territory occupied by the western allies. He knew that there was uncertainty whether to endure, or to enjoy, whatever the near future held. The war was to end soon, that was certain.

He was grateful for his sore throat and aching joints, without them he probably would not have made up his mind. He probably would have been suspended in a web of unbearable uncertainty and procrastination. He was now free, relaxed, and fell fast asleep. When he finally woke up, he looked at his watch. It had stopped, and then he looked out at the street, and the sky. The sun told him it was noon. That eternal clock was always right. His sore throat and aching joints were gone. And he felt well.

Chapter Three

The Earth felt guilty. It wanted to hide. The sun barely showed its face, great spring flagging was going on. Sun-whips cut slices of dust and mud and put golden letters on everything; freedom for the whores, freedom for the saints and freedom of whoredom and saintliness in everybody. Put children in the world, with snake bodies and owl eyes, with weasel minds and bear furs to run and run around in circles until everything burns like in hell. Hell, come and burn us before the soldiers do. Why are soldiers less than men? Why is your brother different in uniform? Is he still your brother? Why is the gun so powerful? It does not kill the enemy, it kills you; it rapes your daughter, your wife, and your mother, living or dead; it destroys your furniture; it robs your house; it kills your dogs. Guns, blue or black kill you.

Great spring flagging was going on.

* **

A few bursts of machine gun fire could be heard at a distance. The sound was faint, almost like imagination. The distant sound expanded into a different dimension; people almost smelled the gunpowder. An occasional deep rumble mixed in as an added variety. It caused resonance in the chests. Nobody knew what it meant. It sounded closer than the machine guns.

The doctor paid little attention to the strange, rumbling noise. From the time when he left his hometown in the fall until now he heard the sounds of war at times for hours without change of the frontline. His nerves were dull, numb or just dormant because he ignored the warning of his ears and let a sense of calmness guide him to the hospital to return to work. He hoped to see Marika. He wanted to tell her about his decision. He wanted to tell her that, when the situation demanded, he would travel west. He imagined that she had the same idea in mind. Her father did, for sure.

The stone faced hospital looked the same. It had not changed while he was gone. There were no new wrinkles, no pimples nor other noticeable changes.

The doctor reported back to his ward. He felt the handshake of his colleagues and noticed the smiling face of his chief. They were glad to see him. The workload was tremendous, and he had been missed for the past three days.

The routine work of the hospital was upside down. No work pattern was recognizable. New ways of thinking were forced upon the doctors and the administration. The patient load in the different departments changed rapidly. Sizeable changes occurred almost hourly. The limited staff was unable to handle the overload. To create a picture of some kind of order, the departments loaned their employees to others to help out. The surgery and outpatient areas needed much extra help particularly after an air raid. The hallways looked like field hospitals at times. Cots lined up, many injured people were sitting on the floor. Everybody was waiting for the magic next; there was no time to write down the names. The chaos, the uncertainty, the injuries were great equalizers.

The younger doctors did not mind switching departments. In spite of great inadequacies, the hospital spirit was excellent. Supplies were low, and the lack of medicines was critical.

The need and desperation created new methods of treatments—excellent at times, a miserable failure at other times. Gonorrhea was wide spread. Many newborns were infected during delivery by their mother's condition. *Ophthalmia neonaturum,* (gonorrheal conjunctivitis) was frequent. Since medicine was not available an unusual treatment was tried. Normal vaginal bacteria of healthy women were transplanted into the eyes of the infected neonate. If it occurred, it usually took three or four days before the infection could be diagnosed, and then it was confirmed by cultures in the transferred bacteria. The results were astonishingly good. Bacillary dysentery in children was a different and very serious problem. The children became dehydrated from high fever and lack of fluids and nourishment. They were given grated apples in hope that it would stop the diarrhea, but it did not work. In some cases a syringe full of blood was drawn from the infant and injected into the muscle. That was thought to stimulate the immune system. No children were saved by that method.

Doctor Nándor's new assignment was to join the pediatric department for a few days. An epidemic of influenza was in the upswing. The department was filled to capacity. New cases were streaming in.

The doctor introduced himself to his new chief, Dr. Szilágyi, a refugee doctor, assistant professor of pediatrics. He presented Sándor the facts without emotions.

"Diphtheria has become a major problem during the past few weeks. As you must know, we have no medication at all. Antiserum is not available. Our treatment is only supportive. We treat the fever, do anything we can to prevent airway obstruction and try to maintain nutrition. As you see we do very little. Our mortality rate is high."

The isolation department of pediatric care was located in a new building a fairly long distance from the central building and in proximity of the huge psychiatric department.

The building was structurally excellent. The rooms were small but the ventilation was very good. It had its own formula room, bacteriology lab, sterilizing equipment and storage areas. There was a pharmacy, desperately empty.

Many small children had pneumonia as well. They were gasping for every breath. The sight of dying within well-decorated, clean walls as opposed to death among the rubbles after a bombing raid was an unforgettable contrast.

"How many die everyday?" Dr. Nándor asked.

"None if we are lucky, but mostly three or four will die."

"Then, we don't save anybody."

"No, nature or God saves some. Nothing is predictable."

"How can war be this cruel and insane?" Dr. Nándor remarked.

"That question has been around for centuries. But János, be careful what you say aloud in public."

"Thanks," he said. Then he continued, "Seeing just one or two of these suffering children is much, but witnessing what goes on with so many is hardly bearable."

The doctor smelled the peculiar sweetish, grayish smell of diphtheria throughout the building. He was to stay on duty all night. The prospects were poor. Four or five children would die by daybreak. The doctor on duty occupied the last room next to the consultation room. Dr. Nándor lay down on the heavily starched white sheet covering the iron frame bed. He tried to go to sleep. Many times during the past years he found himself in situations where nothing was to be done, nothing at all. Whatever was to come had to be accepted. Everything turned out fine, bombings, starvation, and survival.

While he waited for sleep to visit him, he somehow had the notion that this desperate situation with diphtheria could come to an end. When he pronounced the fourth child dead, like a volcanic eruption, a solution, just a possible solution traveled through his paths of thoughts. The morning was right at the doorsteps. He hardly could wait to tell Dr. Szilágyi about it. He met him at the breakfast table.

"Good morning, doctor. I think I can get some diphtheria anti-serum."

Dr. Szilágyi thought that it was an unusual morning greeting but said nothing, he waited.

"I don't know how much and how soon, but if you let me see what I can do, and you can do without me for a day, I think I can get some."

"Well, János, tell me about it." Dr. Szilágyi said softly.

Dr. Nándor remembered that on his way to Szombathely, a few months ago in a small town about 12 or so miles to the east, he was not really sure of the distance, he encountered a large army unit stationed there while waiting to go to Germany. At that time he had gone without food for a day. If that unit had a doctor he may be in luck and could visit with a colleague, perhaps even could get a meal. He inquired; and soon he was received by the military physician. He could not remember his name now or his rank. He was treated with kindness and courtesy. The food was not much, but it tasted heavenly.

His visit with the military doctor was pleasant considering the circumstances. He learned that the unit was to move to Germany, for "training."

"For training, who are they kidding," he said. "It is like teaching somebody to swim in case the frozen river gets rid of the ice. This river is so far gone that even Johnny Weissmüller could not swim it. You know who Johnny Weissmuller is?" Doctor Nándor knew, of course. He remembered what Dr. Szilágyi said and did not comment. Agents provocateurs were everywhere. During his conversation with the military doctor he learned that a large biological supply was stored in what appeared to be an abandoned barn. At that time he did not pay attention to the existence of medical supplies. He had a vague recollection that he saw boxes with diphtheria antiserum.

"As soon as we get to Germany," the military doctor said. "We will have no use for these. We do not know when we are leaving, but we have orders to leave everything here. We will have to move fast and cannot be slowed down with useless materiel."

He was sure, or at least almost sure that the military unit had gone to Germany by now. If they were still there, the military doctor would help. Through his connection with Dr. Nándor and the Health Department, he was sure that he could secure the appropriate papers that might be needed to take possession of the medicines.

Dr. Szilágyi was delighted He was more than willing to let him go. "This is a long shot. I hope you know it. You must know too that you may be killed. We think you will be very close to the frontline. But we really don't know."

János knew. He was willing to take a chance. "I will be careful," he said. "Get going," Dr. Szilágyi responded. He sounded hoarse, his throat felt tight. Dr. Nándor was on his way to the Health Department.

***

The appropriate papers were issued immediately. "You're crazy," he heard. "I know," was the short answer.

He had not seen Marika for days. He wanted to tell her about his trip but mostly he wanted to see her. His feeling for her and the tension he felt about his new enterprise paired up to a peak that was something he never experienced before. He returned to the hospital.

Marika was busy taking inventory and labeling individual medicine bottles and envelopes. A German shipment of medicines just arrived. In a sudden flare up of courage he said, "How would you like to take a trip?"

"A trip . . . where could I go, and why would I want to take a trip? She asked.

He told her about the mission, and suggested that she accompany him. "I know, it is crazy but those dying children," he paused. "We would have to walk about twelve miles one way, but if we start now, we could be back by nightfall."

"I don't know," she hesitated. "We're packed; we could leave for Germany any time, almost any minute. My father doesn't want to wait. He wants to leave now."

"Then it's final. You'll go west."

"Yes. I am sure my father is right. He thinks it is only a question of days, and then the Russians will be in Vienna."

"I believe that too. How can one go before the very last minute as a matter of flight, not emigration?" He asked.

"He obtained some papers."

"Lucky man, provided he does not get caught with them," he said.

"I sure wouldn't want to be in Russian hands with German papers in my pocket. Of course, in your case it wouldn't make any difference because *you* are a woman."

She knew what he meant.

"It is quite dangerous to go east now." She hesitated just a few seconds, then she added. "The frontline is about twenty miles away. It would give us about eight miles distance."

"I have been closer than that once," he interjected.

She continued, "Two small German Panzer units were dispatched last night. They will hold the line for a few days."

"How do you know?" He asked.

"I don't! Ask my father how he knows."

"He does?"

"Yes."

The answer surprised him but he said nothing.

The road out of the city took them past indescribable destruction. They had not realized until now the horrendous effect of the bombings. There was hardly any trace of the railroad station. Freight cars were piled up with their bellies and wheels skyward. A large, specially constructed concrete air raid shelter was completely lifted from the ground. It showed no damage, but was leaning on one edge in a water filled crater. It was a minor miracle. The scene looked like a bleeding, suffering face just in the moment of death. Clothes, furniture, appliances were scattered over a large area. Men, women and even children were digging in the rubble. The air smelled like rotten flesh. Dismembered bodies were still uncovered. A uniformed torso lay beside the road. The pelvis and legs were completely missing. A few people looked at it, and early flies darted upon the decaying body.

They stopped and looked too. They needed to look around. The destruction exerted a magnetic force upon them, tightened their muscles, and directed their vision. They could not help it.

They did not look at each other for a while. They walked as if they were carrying heavy weights. Their backs were tense. Their necks were bent. The corners of their mouths curved downward. Their hands were in fists. They walked at a fast and heavy pace. Their shoulders touched occasionally.

The town was behind them now. They looked back and saw haze or smoke or dust settling on the ruins. The sun was vibrating and piercing.

Suddenly, Marika took János by the hand and started running. He followed her. The scene was like a movie-scene, running for no good reason. It made no sense to him but it was enjoyable. Soon they were warm and short of breath. She was setting the pace. Suddenly, just as she started, she stopped, spun around János a few times. Then she stopped completely, stood in front of him, looked in his eyes. Their clothes touched. Then she asked, "Do you love me?"

János, completely caught by surprise, felt his throat getting warm and scratchy. He turned red. He felt really warm now.

"Yes." he squeezed out. He sounded hoarse. He cleared his throat.

"That's good," she answered.

He knew that it was the wrong comment. Non committal, like . . . "really?" He was disappointed, of course, but he did not let on. Something, suddenly, changed. If there was innocence in their relationship, it now changed to something else. He had to find out.

She started to run again. Now, he chased her. She was taking turns to the right, then to the left. He pretended not to be able to catch up with her. He observed her motions. It was something new, quite pleasant. Finally, she stopped as if exhausted. He knew that she wasn't.

"I caught you," he pronounced. He did not.

They embraced.

During the last few miles they hardly spoke. They felt close. He was surprised at her and himself. She was playful even under these clearly awful circumstances. An intimate feeling developed between them that was both attractive and disturbing, especially after she clearly declared no love for him. János was disturbed but accepted whatever they had. He didn't know what it was.

Marika was unusual, János thought. His analysis told him that ordinarily young women including college students were shy. The man had to make all of the advances, eventually the young woman submitted, but there was a definite, predictable pattern to this.

Marika was not careful, not bashful, and not stiff. In a sense she was unusual. She acted like some of the movie heroines. Deep inside his logical brain he thought that maybe she had experience. He was ashamed for thinking that. Still, there was another factor. She knew too much about German troop movements. He chased that thought away.

Their trip was quite lonely now. They only saw an occasional person out in the field. Their only company was up in the sky and in the grass next to the road. Up high a large formation of bombers moved in an easterly direction. These large bodied silver birds were accompanied by fast moving fighter planes that circled them like the riders with shotguns around wagon trains. "What was there in the east to bomb?" The doctor thought. He did not understand that these bombers already had done their job in the west, and now were returning to their bases in Africa.

Marika and János didn't take shelter. German propaganda frequently spoke of American aerial banditry, claiming that the fighter planes gunned down civilians on the road and in the fields. On one occasion, a milk delivery truck with glistening milk cans was attacked and the driver killed. Such an episode was an exception and was very likely caused by mistaking the shiny cans for military equipment.

At the beginning of the war when airplanes approached, and people were in an open area, they tried to hide wherever they could, under trees, in the grass, or just flat on the ground face down. Now they just kept walking as if on a pleasure trip.

On the roadside many signs of spring established eye contact with them and invaded their senses. Violets were blooming, forming large patches. The air was fragrant. The blades of the grass were sharp, some were silvery. The trees were loaded with small buds ready burst open in a few days. A frog was warming up near a puddle. It plunged in the water as they walked by.

János picked some violets, tied them into a small bundle with the rubber bands he had in his pocket, and gave them to her. She fastened the violets over her left breast and kissed him.

They had more than ten miles behind them—miles of death and resurrection. Two worlds: death was brought about by the war; and resurrection was urged by the spring. Their muscles felt warm and their hearts felt big, as if they were trying to unite with infinity, not with the loathsome present.

They could hear machine gun fire now. There were some single explosions as well. As they got closer to the village they met people hurrying, carrying boxes, and some carried weapons. They were all civilians. Many had Party armbands. There were only a few soldiers.

An elaborate system of trenches sprawled between the small hills on the west side of the village. Heavy concrete blocks fortified the road. There were two cannons pointing to the east, but no soldiers. There were some machine gun nests again without soldiers. The trenches were filled with civilians carrying weapons. Two large concrete blocks towered like monuments on each side of the road creating a bottleneck—presumably to prevent the movement of heavy tanks. The fields were still muddy; heavy armor was confined to the roads.

The absence of soldiers was disturbing and frightening.

A young man about János' age noticed them, and greeted them with his right arm raised, and said, "Kitartás." He did not say, "Éljen Szálasi." If he had, that would have been the official Nyilas Party greeting. He was wearing a dark suit; his trousers were tucked into military boots. He seemed to be in charge.

János explained their mission, and showed him his papers. They were self-explanatory. The details were spelled out. The doctor was to pick up medications, and if he found them to take them back to Szombathely.

"You can not go in there now," the young man said. "The village can fall at any minute."

"Where are the Germans?" János asked.

"On the other side."

"How about our own?"

"They are with them, whatever is left of them."

"You people are all civilians here. What is your job?"

"We will hold the line until the Germans can take up new positions on this side of Szombathely."

"Man, there are no trenches there. No fortifications of any kind, only destruction. The eastern part of the city is just about leveled."

"The young man seemed surprised. János thought he could see a wave of color, gray perhaps marching across his face and over his eyes. It lasted just a fraction of a second then he said, "There will be some by the time they are needed." Then he continued, "Back to you, I have orders not to let anyone in. The village is almost empty. You probably won't find your medicine anyway."

"And I have orders to get the medicine. You saw my papers."

They argued back and forth a little while. It was not a heated argument. It was more or less routine. Arguments had a place in those days. They were lending a new color to a life that was washed over with gray and was saturated with the color of blood. There was a little more to argument than decoration to conversation. At times, graft and argument teamed up.

While they were arguing, the doctor learned that the young man was a law student, who was about to finish his studies, but the war interfered. For some mysterious reason he was not inducted. He volunteered through the Party though he was not a Party member. He wore a Party armband.

"These people here are Party members. Mostly students," he said.

In a little while the doctor's argument, and probably his papers, prevailed. The young man consented.

"I'll tell you what," he said. "I will go in with you. Then if you find the medicine we will see if we get some kind of transportation. It is just about stupid to walk here, and hope to carry back enough medicine to do well. We will find you a wagon and horses, if you find your medicine."

They started to walk again. The young man whose name was István Farago—Pista for short—hurried with them. He carried a submachine gun and some ammunition.

They entered the village. They stepped into a different world. The picture changed rapidly. There were soldiers all over. It seemed that they were stationed in every house. There were machine gun and bazooka units at every corner. Several tanks were hidden under twigs and lumber. German and Hungarian soldiers were everywhere, but seemingly, there was no connection between them. Two armies were fighting a common enemy, shoulder to shoulder, but not together. A few civilians walked around with armbands. It seemed that the population had just vanished. They were either hidden or gone.

"Most of the people fled a few weeks ago. The front has been stationary for almost a month. Little by little almost everybody left. Do you remember where the medicine was stored?" Pista asked.

The doctor remembered the exact place. In a few minutes he located the building.

Nobody paid any attention to Pista and János. The soldiers did not even look at them.

Many just leaned against a wall, smoked and seemingly severed all connection with the outside world. They looked as if they were contemplating. They lived two different lives. One life was on the inside, without interaction with their surroundings, and the other life was characterized by breathing, skin ventilation, and growling empty stomachs. Then they entered a large barn that was now a field kitchen. The air smelled inviting in the building. Large kettles were bubbling. Soldiers were sitting and resting on large wooden boxes.

"Here they are," János cried enthusiastically.

"If they aren't empty."

They were not. The boxes were never opened.

"Aren't we lucky?" The doctor kept up his enthusiasm.

"Hell, you're not lucky yet!" Pista answered. "You'll be lucky, if I find some transportation."

It turned out that the military doctor who was the guardian of the medical supply just left the day before. He wanted to stay and face whatever happened after the fall of the village, but changed his mind and left. It was not clear who went with him. It was assumed that the entire medical unit left. Nobody really knew about anybody else. The soldiers only knew that they had a gun, and that could mean survival. Everything else was hearsay.

Pista organized a cart and horses. In those days everything had to be organized. That word had a new meaning that ranged from stealing to confiscating, from black marketing to just borrowing. All those expressions justified possession.

They loaded their precious cargo and got ready to head west. The gunfire sounded louder now. Some shells fell between the houses. The soldiers did not pay any attention as if they were completely oblivious. They stood, sat, some slept and waited. A soldier does not fight circumstances; he does not judge for himself, unless he is authorized; he waits for orders. Thinking was done at the top. The arms and legs do not ask why, they just deal out punches and kicks. For so much noise, the soldiers were very quiet.

Nobody paid attention to them. They drove as fast as they could. The ground was still wet, there was no dust left behind them. As they reached the trenches at the west side of the village, Pista jumped off the cart and shook hands with them. He looked infinitely sad. Nothing was said.

The road was in a fairly good condition. At some points large piles of gravel were on the roadside apparently ready to be used for repair. Large water filled holes punctured the road for one mile.

They were alone again. János whipped the horses to a slow trot. They were in a hurry. They were smiling again. The gunfire was more distant and seemed to calm down as they left the small village behind and approached Szombathely. They took deep breaths; their diaphragms sank deeply and ventilated their tense lungs. They now realized how scared they really were.

Fear is usually evident before and after. Before the trip they did not realize how close to the front they would have to be. Had they known, they would have never made the trip.

There is hardly anything as pleasant as dissolving fear. It's as if fog was lifting under the gold of the sun. Vanishing fear is like that. When that happened pores would draw tension into the arteries reaching to the fingertips. They change color and start feeling warm. János and Marika felt warm and carefree. Their feeling of freedom and carelessness was tempered by the knowledge that something would happen soon, something only vaguely predictable and ugly.

They entered the city and drove over dirt and ruins.

"What about the horses?" the doctor asked.

"Yes, what about them?"

They had the horses. They were never told what to do with them once they delivered their cargo. They had no idea whose horses they were. Pista just organized them. In the confusion and sounds of war, questions somehow were inappropriate.

"Dr. Szilágyi will love the serum, but what is he going to do with the horses?"

"He?" She asked.

"Well, us."

Now that they almost had a taste of frontline activity, this problem looked hilarious. They laughed and enjoyed their freedom to do so.

János turned serious, and then turned toward Marika.

"Look Marika," he said. "These horses and the buggy could come in handy. You know as well as I do that the time will come, and it is not far that we will have to go to Germany. Why don't we try to take care of them and use them? They will help us make it to the border or even go beyond, if we can find feed for them."

He turned more serious and continued. His voice trembled. "And another thing," he continued, "from now on I would like to stay with you. Who knows?"

"So would I!" She interrupted. She moved closer to him.

Soon they reached the hospital and stopped in front of pediatrics.

Chapter Four

The horses were a short lived sensation on the hospital ground. Within a few hours they became a part of the complex, like the buildings, like the trenches and bunkers. They were there and accepted. Why and how, were questions used in the past, now almost forgotten. Nobody really cared why the horses were there. It was the horse's business, or perhaps somebody else's.

It was late, around midnight when the doctor got off work. He administered diphtheria antiserum for hours. Every child received the right dose. Tomorrow would present a new challenge.

As he headed home on the deserted street his thoughts flew restlessly like moths around a flame. He knew that he would leave for the west soon. He was uncertain what route to take. He needed to look at his map.

He was past the square. The large open space surrounded by tall buildings yawned. It was deserted, and bored. A few days earlier it was the scene of a planned mass meeting in support of the government and the war. It was a failure. The energy of the masses could not be wasted for cheer; it was reserved for self-preservation.

One of the side streets, ordinarily quiet and sleepy was busy. Agitated, hurrying German soldiers were carrying large boxes, typewriters and furniture to the waiting trucks with their motors running. The trucks were lined up, perhaps ten of them. The German military headquarters had been evacuated. He asked one of the soldiers what was going on.

"The Russians broke through," he was told. His heart stood still for a moment, and then he felt its forceful beats in his temples and his throat. It seamed that Szombathely had been given up. The ground that he walked on earlier in the day turned into battle ground, so it seemed.

He started to run. He had to get home in a hurry. There was little time left. The front was moving very close. He knew that no preparations for the defense of the city had been made.

He ran the longest run of his life.

A few Ratas started to drop bombs. People were running in every direction. They paid no attention to each other or to the planes. Chaos engulfed the city, and there was no solid information to lean on. Some horses were racing among the people sharing the general confusion. Suddenly they stopped and stomped their feet. Their mouths dripped foam. The planes used their machine guns now. They produced a high pitched shrill sound, almost like a flute that would never stop playing the same note.

Everybody moved next to the walls. A bomb dropped next to the horses. One horse fell to the ground. Another one just stood with his head down to his knees. His mane fell symmetrically to both sides like a black scarf.

The doctor reached his house. He bundled some documents and some clothes into a bedspread. He folded the corners to the center and tied them. He enclosed a small bag of sugar lumps too. They would supply some energy for a while.

He looked around the room. The books, furniture, and clothes, in the open closets were not aware of him. He had all of his possessions wrapped in the bedspread. In just a few minutes he was heading to the hospital.

Dr. Szilágyi was at the pediatric isolation ward. It looked as if everybody was on duty. Many families of doctors moved into the hospital, presumably it was safer. Everybody thought that the hospital would be a sanctuary when the Russians occupied the city.

Somehow everybody knew that the front had collapsed, and the Russian troops were approaching rapidly. People have an extra sensory perception. At times the results are good; at other times they missed what was obvious.

These perceptions usually do not manifest themselves in the conscious. They accumulate and erupt at some critical time . . . . Great historic events, revolutions can start when pent up emotions and information find their way and explode. Tonight was one of those critical times. People, like swarming bees filled the streets, heading west. There was confusion in the air and on faces. No streetlights were burning. Everybody's fate was in their own hands. People moved about like shadowless shadows.

János said good-bye to Dr. Szilágyi who decided to stay. His family was not with him. His wife and children moved to an area north of the Danube months earlier when the German resistance was still strong. Until now, people believed that Budapest could be successfully defended. Now they knew that it was an illusion and had to be given up.

János took the wagon and the horses and drove across town as fast as he could. He stopped in front of Marika's house. He found nobody there. The family was gone.

There was no time for hesitation. The darkness intensified the sound. The sounds of war now could be identified. One could hear the difference between the sound of the German and Russian machine guns. The German guns sounded like cogwheels biting at high speed; a grinding and low sound. In contrast, the Russian guns were like a high pitched howl perforated by fractions of silence, how many per second was a matter of guess. The sky was bright red on the southeast. The double thuds of the bazooka were frequent and unmistakable. Flashes of lightning burned and split the sky.

The doctor reached the west end of the town and found the road leading to Sopron. Located close to the Austrian border, it served as the capital of the western, German held part of Hungary. That function would end very soon.

The road turned to the northeast then it curved to the northwest. For a few miles the battle noise became very intense. It rocked the ground several times like an earthquake. After he passed the most eastern curve of the road the noise subsided. By daybreak everything was quiet.

The barracks outside the city limit were empty. The buildings were standing at attention. A soldier wearing battle uniform was walking toward town and yelling at the people who were heading west.

"Don't go anywhere," he said. "You are crazy. The Russians will not bother anybody." Nobody paid attention to him.

The confusion was endless and universal. All kinds of makeshift and regular vehicles were moving to the west. The great exodus continued for several hours and for several miles. The darkness yielded to the wakening of the day. Some people gave up and turned around.

The doctor's wagon was loaded with refugees. He picked them up as he progressed. Their feet were hanging over the side. They were sitting on their belongings. The children were sleeping; and their heads bounced on the luggage.

"Where was Marika now?" János asked himself. "Why didn't she wait? Perhaps she tried to get in touch with him at the hospital but they missed each other. Maybe her father had an opportunity to pick up transportation. But, she knew about the horses. They could have traveled together."

The morning was cold. When the sun gathered enough strength to provide a little warmth and some foggy light there were fewer vehicles. The column was shorter. The old major and his wife stood on the roadside holding on to a bicycle. There was one large suitcase tied to the luggage rack. They were standing; their strength was gone. They did not ask for a ride. They saw that the doctor's wagon was loaded to capacity. A little while later a military truck picked them up.

A few miles to the north they saw the same couple again. They were walking holding on to the bike. The truck was parked beside the road, no more a part of the war, probably waiting for the Russians.

A little after daybreak they reached the outskirts of Sopron. They met confusion and disarray. Columns of horse dawn vehicles were lined up for miles. The traffic came to a complete halt. János heard that the columns have not moved for hours. The explanations were many.

"German troops are moving though Sopron. We have to wait for them," somebody suggested when he inquired.

"They are fixing the bridge at the border. It was blown up during the night."

He heard more explanations that were based mostly in imaginative speculation, nothing else.

Wagons, carts, and trucks were loaded to capacity. The vehicles looked like piles of garbage guarded by people who were sitting on top of the junk. Most of these people were refugees, settled in the west for what they thought would be only a temporary inconvenience and could go back after a German victory.

Now they were moving west again with different plans and hopes. They found that suitcases were not practical. They were too heavy, their shape was impractical. They did not fit into tight spaces. Improvised bundles were more practical. Their belongings were wrapped in bedspreads, sheets and blankets. They showed irregular bulges.

The people wore several sets of clothes. Men wore two, three trousers and several sweaters. The excessive clothing made their heads and faces small. Precious luggage space was saved that way. Everybody was restless. Their movements represented overcompensation for exhaustion and frustration. To that was added the uncertainty of the immediate and distant future. If they made it to Germany and the war ended would the winning powers repatriate them, hand them over to the Russians?

There was general restlessness. The men were pacing around the vehicle. Some walked ahead twenty or thirty wagon lengths to seek information. What they learned showed on their facial expressions upon their return, some were stone-faced and excessively somber, some others grinned with confidence. "It will be only minutes," one asserted.

"In just a little while the border will be open." others said.

The morning was cold. The sun shone brightly. In sunshine, the stress and possible major disappointment were easier to take. In this cold, but bright morning, nature provided a spectacle that the refugees witnessed with fascination. Most of them never saw anything like this;

and they would never see this again. Some people considered it a sign of their approaching doom.

An enormous number of crows circled over an open field that was cut into sections by trenches. Civilians carrying guns and machine guns were wandering around aimlessly. They wore black clothes, some had arm bands. They looked like ants running around confused. Above them, the crows formed a column that reached into the endless height of the sky. The base of this spectacular column that looked more like a pyramid was about a mile across, not dense with the flying birds. Higher up the base narrowed and the birds circled closer to the center. At the top there were only a few birds fighting until one started to fall like a torn rag.

In the center, the birds fought all alone. They made an eerie whining noise. There were many dead birds on the ground. The birds circling on the outside were cheering on the ones fighting in the center. The fallen birds, if they were alive, were attacked on the ground and were virtually torn apart. This was a first class massacre that depicted what was going on all over the world. The birds had their own world. They ignored the men in and around the trenches.

The people and vehicles stranded on the road were another spectacle witnessed by the universe. Watching the fighting and dying crows made some women hysterical. Some screamed and animated the skirmish of life that was frighteningly out of hand.

After about an hour of waiting and getting nowhere, the doctor decided to abandon his wagon and horses. He turned over the team to a young chemist with a lovely wife and two small children. He took his bundle with some of his clothes and sugar and started to walk. He looked in each vehicle hoping to see Marika.

He passed an endless number of carts and wagons, and as he got closer to the city he heard that some of the wagons had been stranded for more than forty-eight hours. The horses didn't have any feed, some people started to feel early starvation. Those who had food shared it with the others.

The doctor had no difficulty getting around in this chaos of horses, vehicles and people. He was laughed at, at times, because he walked. They assured him that he would never be able to get to Germany because only soldiers with their families would be permitted to pass. On this road that was clogged, and was leading nowhere, a new class of people emerged, a class of paper carriers. Many had some sort of German documents that would allow them free passage into Germany. At this point in time their papers were worthless, but they didn't know that.

He had never been to Sopron before. He had no idea where he was headed, or how he was to get out of the city, or how to get across the border and enter Germany. The border meant something mysterious to him, something that provided strength and security. A little later he learned that the marks on the map had no meaning at all. In this war geographical limits meant no more than thresholds of houses.

For the next few months the Russians would go in and out without regards to nations or individuals. States and families would be suspended. Everything and everybody, and in particular women, would become Russian property. When Milovan Djilas, Tito's friend spoke with Stalin about the outrageous behavior of the occupying soldiers, Stalin allegedly said, "So, they have a little fun with women, but they fight the Germans." All this went on until the western winds became strong.

The city square was jammed with German military vehicles, mostly trucks. The soldiers stood next to their vehicles. Most trucks were empty.

The canvas flaps were waving in the wind. Civilians were hurrying in every direction. Every person was carrying something. They looked like parts of a disturbed anthill. Nobody walked at a normal pace. Everybody rushed . . . with strained muscles, and simple-minded facial expressions . . . with an internal drive and importance. Sophistication completely disappeared. It looked and felt as if fright was settling on the entire city.

He reached the north edge of the city. He stopped and turned around. A conglomeration of aimless existence moved in human waves everywhere. All of the streets were clogged. There wasn't any orderly, or organized traffic.

As he looked he realized for the first time that the hardly imaginable litter and destruction symbolized a decaying and crumbling nation. This was the output of a colossal grinder that consumed Hungary. Hungary as he knew and loved it existed no more. Memory took a somber dive; it became fragmented and was later reconstructed by history writers, for another generation to read, not necessarily for them to believe.

The sky was clear. It was twelve noon. A church bell started to ring like on any normal day at noon commemorating the victory of Hunyadi over the Turks hundreds of years ago.

He saw a column of German military vehicles, mostly trucks that stood isolated and seemed abandoned. One young soldier sat on the running board of one of the vehicles. His head rested on his thigh. He wore no hat. He was blond like so many Germans. His uniform was clean and his boots were polished. The doctor approached the vehicle. The way these trucks were lined up suggested to him that they may be ready to pull out. The head of the column was quite a distance away in one of the side streets.

Four people hurried to the rear of one of the trucks and started to load oil paintings, a large wooden easel, and several oblong wooden boxes that seemed quite heavy.

Soon the loading was completed and the first couple, a woman about fifty, and a man a little older, took seats on the boxes. The second, an elderly couple remained standing next to the truck. They were very upset, kept wiping their tears, then after some hesitation they left, disappearing among the vehicles.

The couple in the truck told János that the column would move on to the west within an hour. This was very good news. Some German soldiers returned to their vehicles now. János picked a young man in a clean lieutenant's uniform to inquire about the possibility of a lift to Germany. He chose the most polite way to frame a question the way he learned at school.

It went like this, "Excuse me for disturbing you. Would there be a possibility to travel with you to Germany?" His German was good enough for the lieutenant to understand. He was friendly and very much to the point. What he said was frightening for two reasons.

First, this was the first time that he heard a German admit that they had difficulties. Even defeat after defeat at the various frontlines, official Germany never admitted any problems. More than that, what he said was frightening.

"We are completely out of gasoline, but there is a chance that we might trade some for food. You are welcome to join us."

He climbed up into the back of the truck that was occupied by the woman and her older husband.

He learned that the lady was an artist of excellent reputation. She and her husband lived on an estate in Sopron. They considered leaving for Germany only temporarily and intended to be back after the war. They did not say, "when the war was won," only that "when it was over." The other couple with them had been their servants. They were to take care of the estate in their absence.

There was a great deal of naiveté in what they said and in the manner they said it. The doctor could easily understand the natural attachment of an artist to his work.

Nevertheless the constant talk about her paintings was completely out of line. She spoke of German art experts who were enthusiastic about her work and the amount of money she received for one of her flower paintings.

"A worthless piece of paper," János thought, but said nothing. He just nodded and did not start any conversation.

The two people talked unceasingly either to each other or to him.

At one point their conversation sent electric shocks through his spine. She said to her husband "I wonder how the Magyars are doing. I understand they were in Szombathely. They must be going through here if they are leaving for Germany. On the other hand they may just go through Graz."

"Did you say Magyar?" He almost shouted.

A short conversation followed to make sure that both parties knew the same Magyars. There was no question about it. These people knew Marika. A few years ago she even spent a summer with them.

"She is such a wonderful girl," he said. "She was a little wild. Her father could not control her so he sent her to us. We had no children. We were much younger than the Magyars. Of course we were not sure that we would understand Marika better than her father or her mother."

He listened. He did tell them about their work at the hospital, but he did not say anything about their relationship that he thought was love.

The artist, whose married name was Fekete, used to be a Magyar and was in some way related to Marika's father.

Mr. Fekete owned a huge estate similar to the one the Magyar's owned near Debrecen. The two families spent time together in the capital where they met often for happy weekends.

János wanted to know more about Marika, particularly about her wildness, but was afraid to ask.

In approximately one hour the gasoline was secured and the column started to move. They were fairly comfortable in the truck and were surprised that the Germans did not pay attention to them at all. They completely ignored them as if they were nonexistent.

The square lay on a slight slope. As they drove higher he was able to look down and able to see the hopelessness of the situation; he saw thousands of people far away from home, away from anything that ever meant something to them stranded in a strange city just a stone's throw distance from the frontline. Something filled the air that smelled like a storm coming. The lightning sat there loosely . . . on everybody's shoulders . . . that sagged like bridges with an overload.

This picture was the last one he remembered of Hungary. This was the last thing his eyes scooped up and preserved. The motors purred and the wheels swished westward.

Huge holes yawned along the road guarded by piles of dirt that looked like anteater's castles. The trucks hurried by them. They crossed a bridge that was to be blown up in a few seconds. After the bridge came a bare reddish-yellow land. No trees, no shrubs, not even a blade of grass. The trucks kept rolling. There was desolation from horizon to horizon. Quite suddenly the trucks stopped. The soldiers jumped out, threw their helmets in the air and hugged each other. *"Heimat, Heimat, Deutschland, Deutschland."*

Chapter Five

This spontaneous primitive celebration took only a few minutes. It was like a quick shower in the spring coldness, warm and refreshing. It lasted just enough to put pink color into the soldier's faces and a prickling heat inside their blood.

The bridge blew up with a thunderous light. It looked as if fingers reaching to the sky were balancing black poles of dirt and dust. The road to the east was closed behind them. Thousands waiting in Sopron to gain passage to Germany were now stranded. The German army gave up Hungary.

The soldiers jumped back into their trucks. They still paid no attention to their Hungarian passengers who witnessed their grotesque celebration and the destruction of the bridge.

The trucks started to move again. They moved disconcerted on the land that witnessed their effort, but was neutral like the air. This area belonged officially to Germany now but it looked different than any land kissed by the sand and the rain. There were farmhouses along the road. Their white washed faces smiled peacefully. Their window eyes, located usually on both sides of the entrance, blinked and winked. The chimneys smoked with thick gray haze that rose straight up like virtues.

Many farmers spoke Hungarian here. This land belonged to Hungary until the treaty of Trianon. It kept many of its Hungarian characteristics during the twenty-seven years of Austrian and German rule. Since the Anschluss, a certain amount of mechanization took place. More farm equipment was visible, but that did not change the character of the area.

The land was just like the territories east of here. Orchards and farms lay quietly, almost dormant in peaceful unity. There was nothing different about this land from any other part of the world. This piece of land with its houses, roads, trees could represent the east as well as the west. Externally there was nothing that made this little strip of Austria remarkable. The doctor had a strange feeling, a quality that he could not describe. He knew that this feeling like so many others would vanish with the flow of time. It was there now. This was like a wanting to sit down on a hill and gaze into the distance. The feeling was like the quality of a shelter. He knew that this feeling was self-deceit. Germany was dead. There was only one alternative, build on the ruins whenever and wherever it became possible. He still had a choice of location. The trucks rolled to the west. The border disappeared. He looked at the Feketes. They were asleep.

Gradually some of the trucks became hot and hungry, particularly the ones that were not running on gasoline. Because of the great shortage of liquid fuel, the Germans converted some of their trucks to gas engines. The gas was obtained from large containers that were mounted to the right side of the vehicle just ahead of the door. Wood blocs, similar to children's building blocks filled these containers. Underneath them fire was burning. The source of this fire was not evident. In the large containers dry distillation of the wood took place and produced gases that powered the converted motors. The trucks stopped now and fresh wooden blocks were filled into the containers.

The doctor took advantage of this break and hurried to a nearby farmhouse in the hope of obtaining some food. His short expedition was futile. The farmer said no. He did not explain, he just said no. János went back to the trucks. Soon the travel continued. The weather was cold but friendly. The soldiers seemed more relaxed. They were singing now some sad sounding songs. The motors drowned out most of the singing. The wind carried some fractions of the tunes.

"Foreign songs always sound sad," he thought.

The Germans were quite friendly now. They were anxious to get home. They spoke freely about their defeat. They hoped to avoid being prisoners of war. They knew that when they were defeated they would be just that. When would they be soldiers no longer? Probably today.

He learned that in the next village they would stop. They were now approximately thirty miles inside Germany. The trucks would pick up some ammunition and head back east. He felt uneasy about the fate of these young soldiers. They were younger than he. He almost could visualize their immediate future. He felt sorry for them. The column stopped.

He had not spoken with the Feketes. There was a silence between them, a silence that communicated and was meaningful. He felt a strange affection for them. That made him uncomfortable. He could not explain it. He thought about it, then, after a while, he shrugged his shoulders. They got off the truck.

Bewildered, the Feketes asked, "What now?"

In these crowded events, questions came up with irregularity but with great frequency. There was never a satisfactory answer based on some certainty. He could not answer them. He asked the same question from himself. The answer came as a flood of visions, hopes and possibilities. At that point in time that was all anybody had. He was thinking again of those crowds stranded in Sopron. They too had vision, but it turned into darkness. Indeed entire Hungary experienced darkness that was to continue.

His vision landed him far west from here. That gave him energy. He needed to say something to the Feketes. They too were under the influence of something poorly defined. Its content was kept going; the farther west the better, far enough to a point that the Russians cannot reach.

All around them the Austrians went about their business without hurrying seemingly unaware of the happenings in the east. The shops were open. The show windows displayed all kinds of merchandise. People went in an out of the stores carrying bags presumably food. To János this was a painful sight. In Hungary, the land of plenty, food was scarce, at least in the western territories during the past few months. Here, just a few miles from the Hungarian border there seemed no shortage. Of course, everything was rationed, but it was available. Before the Germans occupied Hungary, and were fighting in Poland, and the Ukraine, the rumor was that the Germans confiscated large amounts of perishables and nonperishables. Could what was seen here have originated in Hungary?

A few hours earlier, when he was looking toward the border that he left behind, his skin flattened like a lake when the wind gives up and dies. Now he felt different. He was inside Germany. He had no passport. He knew nobody. He was an alien, an *Ausländer*. He knew about Hitler's views concerning race. He was not a member of the *Herrenrasse*. He was an inferior creature who just entered Germany, an intruder. He felt miserable and insecure but soon his logic chased away these thoughts. If he was undesirable, "So what?" "They probably will stick me in a uniform," he thought. "In that case my fate will not be worse that that of millions." That gave him peace of mind. He felt the war now. He immersed into the ocean of mass killings, and at least, in his thoughts, he faced whatever was to come.

He stood in an austere, narrow street with his face toward Moscow. His back was turned to London. He watched the German speaking people of middle Europe. He was in a daze. As he absorbed the magnitude of the global war he was nearly unconscious, but still registering everything sharply. At the end of the street a line of military trucks presented a curious sight. While they were military trucks, their cargo was everything but military. He could see: sewing machines, bundles, mattresses, birdcages, kitchen utensils, all kinds of civilian articles. Men, women, children, young and old conglomerated around the trucks and piled heaps of what seemed to be junk, high in a collection of disorder. Men wearing yellowish uniforms were in good spirits and directed traffic and helped people.

The doctor recalled this freely flowing consciousness from the horizons of Europe into this small Austrian village and into his own brain. He had to find out what was going on. He knew that asking too many questions was not fashionable and was quite impractical. He walked along the trucks avoiding the little children running around, observed what he could and finally asked a friendly looking helper what was going on. The uniformed men were members of the TODT organization that was evacuating the ones who wanted to leave. They were scheduled to take off soon.

The people around the trucks were anxious. They held on to their prized possessions, which probably were rescued from attics and basements, quite similar to memories that quite suddenly could surface in minutes when there was a dire need. They were bundled up in warm clothes. These people were ready to leave. There was another group that obviously intended to stay. They visited the stores and presumably carried supplies. These two groups had one thing in common. They held onto something that was going to be useful in the future. Food and suitcases were in competition.

The group of people around the trucks kept an eye on their belongings piled high. The village was evacuated.

The others who obviously decided to stay walked now at an increased speed as if wanting to beat an imaginary clock. They accepted the inevitable. The Russian troops were now just about twenty miles away. These people accepted the future without trying to influence it. They had a different kind of hope. They hoped that there was a force that did not even have a name. This hope was a combination of things, holding on to the soil, suggesting to them that history repeats itself, and knowing sunshine will follow the clouds. That has been the history of Burgenland, a strip of land between east and west.

Throughout the many years of history Europe was threatened over and over by marauding troops from the east. They worked their way to the west until they reached the eastern part of Austria. All their attacks and efforts crumbled in this narrow strip of land and before the walls of Vienna, the mighty queen of the Danube. There was no hope that this could happen again. On the other hand every destruction and misery was followed by revival and rebuilding. These were the thoughts of those who stayed.

The houses in this region looked different. They were taller and had prominent gables. They looked pretty much alike interrupted by tall factory-like buildings. People were hurrying in and out of them. The trucks were lined up in front of them.

János learned that when the TODT organization leaves a city, any city at all, the railroads and major arteries of traffic would be blown up. He had no idea what the TODT organization was, but found out that it had something to do with the building of the Siegfried Line.

He returned to the spot where he left the Feketes. They were sitting on a large wooden box. The paintings were leaning against the house with their face facing the wall. Only a small oil painting in gold frame looked up.

It was approximately 4:00 PM in the afternoon. The sun was sitting low, the shadows were getting longer. They made the air colder. The rays of the sun fell on the painting in the gold frame and formed a halo around the delicate head of a little girl. He thought that the little painting was beautiful. He vaguely imagined that the picture might represent the Marika of some fifteen years ago. He looked but made no comment.

"The TODT organization is leaving soon," he said. "We will have to hurry. We might find a corner on one of the trucks. There will be no transportation out of the city after they leave."

"Oh yes. There will be," Fekete answered. "The Russians will not get here at least for one week. I think we had better look for some place to stay tonight. But if you want to leave . . . ."

János said he would and said good-bye.

He turned around to hurry to the trucks when Mrs. Fekete called him. "Dr. Nándor, would you accept this picture as a present? We will have trouble transporting it anyway." She gave him the picture of the familiar looking girl.

He smiled; he thanked her, and then hurried along. He had trouble hauling his bundle, now he had the picture. Just as he climbed up in one of the trucks the column began to move. Nobody said a word when he climbed up. They just moved a little to make him a place. He sat on a piece of luggage. He held his bundle and his picture on his lap.

The trucks were loaded to capacity with luggage and with people. They were sitting on their belongings, close to each other with their shoulders and backs touching. There wasn't a square inch of free space. The doctor sat on the corner of a box, on perhaps a square foot of surface. It was at the edge of the truck bed. János was able to dangle his feet. He had an advantage over those who sat in the middle. To his right sat a middle-aged man wearing a Tiroler hat with a feather. He had a rugged weather beaten face. His mustache had started to turn gray and ended in two sharp heavily waxed points; he had a typically Austrian-

Hungarian face ornament. On his left sat a young woman with short blond hair. Her complexion was very fair; her eyes were blue. She was bundled up in an overcoat and a heavy scarf. Nobody spoke a word. The faces and expressions were as many as the people. They expressed deep emotions. Their silence was interrupted occasionally by children squealing.

The trucks hugged the road on the edge of a narrow flat land that extended on the right. On the left there was a river. Beyond the river trees were scattered in no particular system or order. They seemed to be "volunteer" trees. There was very little sign of spring here. The ground was dry and there was no grass to be seen, just some dried up weeds, remnants of the winter. The landscape was monochromatic with few clusters of houses. The bright roofs and the white walls overcame the monotony.

The uniformity of the landscape paired up with the monotony of the overworked motors. Against that background János noticed a sign that he never witnessed that early in the springtime. The sun was almost gone now. Cold fog settled near the ground. The chimneys of the house puffed like pipes. There was no breeze. On the right on the top of a chimney on a three story house he noticed the silhouette of a pair of storks. They came home early from their winter trip. They were the first sign of spring in this part of the world. The darkness did not let their color penetrate, but their shape was there. Their backs formed two humps, their tails were pointing down. Their necks were in the resting position buried into their chests. From their chests long feathers were hanging. Their stilt-legs showed a slight bend in their knees. That vision lasted only a few seconds. The trucks chased the spring away. Winter returned with the darkness. This was his second experience with birds today. One was a sign of spring and germination of life, the other was the crows, a sign of death and decay.

The evening was cold. The stars were shining sparingly like always when it is cold. The trucks now began to climb. The trees were closer to the road. Low branches occasionally scraped the trucks and the passengers. The moon was elsewhere and the darkness was heavy. Only the eastern sky lit up and flickered. It was a silent flicker. The front was now at a distance. Against the flickering sky one could see the humps of hills and mountains. The road was now curvy. The passengers felt the upgrade hill. The overloaded trucks cried.

Several hours passed. The cold and monotony invaded their brains and muscles. Gravity got ahold of them and pulled and pulled and pulled. It started with their eyelids.

The slowly evolving slumber was suddenly interrupted by the sound of motors overhead. Nerves were activated. Muscles were electrified. Bodies became light. It became quiet under the hood of the trucks and the headlights went out. There was no need for command. Without rehearsal the passengers jumped off the trucks to take cover under the nearby trees. Several airplanes flew around the column several times. They discharged a few rounds from their machine guns, and then they were gone.

There were no casualties.

The people climbed back into the trucks. Everybody found his own spot. The journey continued.

Taking into account the time spent and the presumed speed of the trucks, Doctor Nándor estimated that they were about seventy miles into Austria. The trucks moved very slow negotiating a steep slope. It was probably 10:00 or 11:00 at night. "I hope there is no avalanche ahead," said the man on his right. The doctor listened. His German was fair, so he understood. "This time of the year the roads over the mountains are impassable," the man continued. "I hope we will not have to turn back."

The woman on his left expressed her feelings, "I guess they know what they are doing. They would not waste time if they were not sure that everything ahead was fine."

"Who knows?" The man answered.

The doctor did not know the feelings and sentiments of his fellow travelers, he just uttered some, "hmm, hmm." He thought that it was wise not to reveal his identity and nationality.

Other people joined the conversation. The time went faster that way. It was good because it was quite cold. It was between eleven and midnight when the column halted. Spots of snow formed white cold faces beside the road. There were patches of ice.

For about an hour or so there was great confusion, which cooled and warmed the air and spirits alternately. Almost everybody got off the trucks and hopped and jumped to keep warm. Some never quit talking.

The doctor was not sure what the confusion and conversations were all about. He judged that he was the only Hungarian in the crowd. He was not afraid to reveal this fact, but he was not too anxious either. He did not join the conversation. He just kept to himself. He hopped on one leg, then on the other. He found that soothing and practical since he was stiff from freezing and sleeplessness. He concluded that the road ahead was blocked by snow. They would have to turn around, go back to where they started, turn north, pass through Wiener Neustadt, turn west again, and go on to St. Pölten. This was very bad news.

The route crossing the mountains was selected originally because Wiener Neustadt was considered unsafe due to the rapidly advancing Russians approaching from the north. Earlier in the afternoon the rumor was that the city would fall anytime. Now there was no other choice, they had to try to make it through that endangered city.

The warm feeling of security was gone now. Earlier, about ten hours ago he let his feelings deceive his logic. He let his skin breath and soothe the wrinkles and pores when the bridge was blown up behind him. What he did not know was that the Russians were making progress on the north and were closing in on Vienna. The TODT organization, therefore, headed toward a small mountain pass much more south. Now there was no other alternative, but to take a chance now when the success of the enterprise was questionable.

The trucks turned around and began rolling quietly down hill. This particular time of the night has a unique, recognizable quality. It can be perceived by a peculiar smell, by the position of the stars that announce that daybreak is inevitably coming. This feeling developed rapidly in everybody. Nobody dozed except the children who were bundled up in heavy blankets to protect their dreaming hearts. There was another reason for feeling the inevitable. The sky was blood red in the northeast. The mountain with its eternal shadows obstructed the base of this red glow that was reaching high in the sky and gave good basis for guesses and conclusions. It was the opinion that Vienna was burning in the inferno of the war.

By the time they saw the friendly green river again they heard loud rumblings; machine guns could be clearly heard. The noise was unmistakable.

Nobody said a word. You almost could hear the rhythm of their racing hearts. As the road turned, their eyes were glued first to the northeast, then to the north, and finally to the east. Nobody counted the minutes. Time was judged by the speed of the trucks and the location of the blood stained sky. Then the frightening vision disappeared.

Wiener Neustadt seemed deserted. Large gray stone buildings shook, the streets were twitching, and the sidewalks cracked. An occasional window shattered.

The color of the city was unbelievably gray. No lights anywhere. Ordinarily, in the city at daybreak one could hear if nothing else barked and howled, not now. Wiener Neustadt had no heart, no digestion. It was, perhaps, just dormant.

There were no soldiers anywhere.

When they reached the open field at the west of the city they felt a few warm fragments of air. The air in the city was stiff and frozen. Life left it and now was waiting for whatever was to come.

***

Death is obvious. Animals and humans recognize it under any kind of conditions.

The medical student who for the first time in his career was called upon to diagnose death does not make a mistake. The death mask unmistakably announces, "I am dead."

There was something else a dead body signals, "I am dead, mourn over me."

Ever since the beginning, time and space have obeyed. Mourning has been a part of human life and emotion. Mourning has been a sacred property of survivors and grief has been a proud heritage.

There was a great variety to mourning and grief. Those two were as identical as laughing and hurting inside a flaming heart. Mourning was cultural; grief was animal. There was hardly ever lack of both. One was always present when an individual left for an unknown destination after death, except in war when the so-called civilized thinking was suspended.

***

The sun began its notorious teasing of the earth and the earth kept turning so as not to be burned. The trucks rolled proudly toward the west, south of the Danube. The highway was good, wide and traveled. The traffic moved in both directions. Large columns of trucks moved west; an occasional vehicle was eastbound. János got used quickly to the keep right, regulation. In Hungary the traffic moved on the left side of the road. Large signs of "Balra Hajts," warned the drivers.

The passengers noticed another traffic that moved slowly on foot on both sides of the highway. It moved in a very long file.

There was a chain of events that looked like this. The unknown mystifies. The mystery is dispelled by guesses. The guesses are usually wrong. Halfway consciously and halfway unconsciously the doctor was aware of this. He simply did not take a guess while looking at the long line of creatures trembling and walking slowly to the west.

They wore green uniforms, the kind that some Russian prisoners of war wore in Szombathely. Their shoes were extremely large; they seemed to dictate the pace and point the way to be followed by hanging arms, drooped shoulders, and buckled knees. It looked like every man was on his own. Nobody spoke. None wore an overcoat and a few had caps that were still recognizable as such. They were carrying nothing in their hands. They looked neither to the right nor to the left. They mostly watched the ground that was gray and dusty and at times yellow. They must have been prisoners of war, but there were no guards.

Every ten feet or so a body in the same green uniform lay across the lone path, or was hanging into the roadside ditch. Many lay there in bizarre positions. Their necks were flexed, probably broken. Their arms were twisted above their heads or under their chests.

Nobody rests in these positions. These people were dead. The dead and the walking formed a unit. That was the only sign of belonging. This was a strangely odd unity. The living paid no attention to the dead. They stepped over the bodies, or wore a path around them. The weight of their shoes showed them the direction.

There was no mourning. There was no grief. The trucks rolled by without curiosity. The motors just did their jobs. Even the passengers were not curious. Everybody accepted the picture of a long line that was fading into the distance. This picture was the result of something, over which they had no power. The doctor did not have a feeling about this one way or the other. His tiredness made him neutral.

A little in front of him sat a young man with a little boy; both appeared tired. No woman sat with them.

"What are those men doing on the roadside, father? The boy asked.

"Just going west."

"Like us?"

"Yes."

"And those lying down?"

"They're going west too."

"No, father, they are not now. What are they doing now?" He sounded inpatient and searched his father's face.

"Now son, now they rest," he answered.

***

The trucks like rivers flowed with great satisfaction. The motors were warm and their exhaust fumes vibrated to be swallowed by the next vehicle. Here the bridges were guarded and were presumably ready to be blown up when the enemy set foot on their cracked back.

An outline of a town showed up in the distance, got larger and became alive when the trucks negotiated street corners and came to a halt at the railroad station.

"Like a dream," the doctor thought. The same picture, people were hurrying, carrying essentials, rejecting sentimental feelings, and saving only what mattered, only things essential for survival. Fight for survival is cruel. There is no place for soft emotions.

Nobody paid attention to the trucks. All attention was focused on the train, which puffed white steam like a rich uncle in your den puffing on his pipe before signing his will in your favor, the good uncle with a heart.

The train represented heart, safety, reason, and just about everything that was still reality in the spring of 1945. It was the last train leaving this territory, which was to be given to the enemy. The town was being evacuated.

The doctor did not ask any questions. He gathered his bundles and hurried to be swallowed by the warm guts of the train. He felt the rumble of steel rubbing against steel. His knees started to feel week and perspiration trickled down his spine. He felt faint.

The train labored, its black smoke rolled to the east. It moved noisily to the west. It operated on its own power independently from the movements of statesmen, nations, destruction, and history. Its power meant life. It's hot steam filled belly meant gestation.

In the warmth of the ice cold unheated train thoughts were vibrating freely and almost settled on the lips to explore the unknown ahead. The unknown is cruel; it wraps the heart with caps of gleaming ice that sends chills along the arteries, and turns the nerves into paralyzed ropes. It converts the human skin into dried out parchment that is void of life and lacks the radiant heat that makes us alive. Free thoughts of dried lips and limp lifeless bodies came alive and were felt across the compartment.

The end was not here yet. Many wished it would stay away forever. Even without an end, a beginning was fermenting to bring something new, to build, generate and absolve the world of its present sense, warm up its skin so it may turn into sunshine and milk.

The train's power was inexhaustible. Its whistle could not be heard at the frontline now. It labored its way along rivers, across bridges, next to roads with backs abused by wheels, and wheels, and more wheels.

Motor vehicles were lined up for miles. Only the sun knew what happened to them. It watched daily from their birth on.

Inside the train there was safety. There was protection. The steel frame and the wooden shell of the cars surrounded the doctor like flesh, and the soothing water of the womb.

Many times in this quest for safety humans long for the womb. It was where it started, in the warmth of the female body where there was peace. The train was like motherly peace.

Darkness crept in. No lights were on in the train. Hot sparks from the engine flew by the window painting lines and dots against the sky. Their code remained a secret.

There were no lights outside. Houses, villages, and towns slept with blankets pulled over their heads. Their shiny eyes were closed. They would open again when the sky got its color back.

The doctor leaned against the boards of the small compartment. He felt pressure against his spine. His knees felt like sponges. They felt like enlarging tissues. They were pushing his bones apart. His toes tingled strangely. His eyes were closed and he moved his toes to keep awake.

In the distance, in the south, hundreds of bright lights burned. At the same time light beams chased each other.

"They keep prisoners there," somebody said. The Amis know not to bomb. The lights keep them away."

The Amis, unchallenged masters of the air just like the Germans were years ago. "Times have changed," the doctor concluded and closed his eyes again. The train stopped several times. Nobody got off; nobody got on. The tracks were damaged and that was the general conclusion. Of course nobody really knew.

To avoid knowledge is an art that pays off when political pots boil. Reaping the silent senses of the words can become a great asset.

After three hours the train scratched, stretched, and then again sucked in the air from the west. A few more short stops during the night and the black turned to gray without delay.

Chapter Six

The military hospital in Passau looked at the rolling waters of the Danube as if saying, you were the only thing going east without hesitation and fear. You were without hate too. Your nation had not changed. History did not alter you. Your slim powerful body stretched from the Black Forest to the Black Sea had withstood history without a goose bump. You faced the hunters years ago. You welcomed Attila a thousand years ago. Your southern waters may even have been carrying molecules from his body at rest somewhere in one of your tributaries. You warned the Turks to drop their swords and retreat. You diluted their blood, which richly nourished you over centuries of fierce fighting. You didn't get sick. Patiently you traveled through time washing away the doubt, sweat and blood of many nations. You were very busy. Remember that was 1945.

Heinrich Wolfgang Gottlieb watched the river. He was motionless. His face was like a mask, a rigid plaster. Soft, cool perspiration found its way down his neck and down his face.

His right temple was clear. The clotted blood that covered it when he collapsed in Szombathely had been removed. There was no scar. The skin was not broken. There was no sign of bleeding. Was it his blood? The doctors did not think that it was.

After he was picked up from the sidewalk in Szombathely the speeding ambulance joined a column of military vehicles heading west. When they reached Passau, he was placed into a clean comfortable bed in the military hospital. A huge red cross painted on the roof of the building appealed to the American Air Force.

The plain white sheets caused him to open his eyes but his lips remained still and closed. No word was said. Not one expression changed his face. Not a single muscle moved, except his pupils and his eyelids. They converted him into a leaving creature. Lifelessly he lay with his eyes open and his heart beating.

For three days he laid there, and then he said, "A white deer, white as snow, over the meadow it runs. The air smells good. The grass is tall. The blades are clean. The rivers are blue and the water is sweet. The boys carry bows and arrows. They run like the deer. Their hair is black. Their eyes are glowing and their nostrils are white. They follow the deer across strange lands. There is music in the air."

"This is my land," one of the boys says. "The deer lead us here brother." The other boy turned his back and headed to the east.

Heinrich fell back. His head was bouncing on the pillow.

"He is hallucinating," his doctor said, making a note in his record. "War can do this to you," he continued. "War does not produce only death and heroes. We have our in-betweens. Heinrich is one of them."

***

The brakes took a strong hold on the tracks. The train whined and sparks landed on the crippled frozen ground. It was cold again. The station welcomed the nearly exhausted train.

The passengers filed out of the train and disappeared among the ruins. The station was destroyed, pulverized to the bones. Bent tracks curved like giant ribs creating huge cavities enclosing bricks, glass, and frozen mud. Bomb craters were seen everywhere.

Just seven years ago, perhaps on this very day, the night was warmed by torches carried by singing marchers hailing the Führer. With the grinding of heavy military machines, the invading German army resounded across the Danube, and then eyes began to glow, and faces began to smile. People carried flowers to greet the Germans. Austria was ready to greet the son of Braunau Am Inn, Adolph Hitler.

When the whinnying of the war horses was heard across the English Channel, wrinkles popped up on foreheads and conference tables were busy day and night. The same sound in two different places. The receptors were different. The doctor stepped out of the train carrying his luggage. There was no gate. Nobody wanted to see his ticket; he did not have one anyway. He followed the other people. Where was he to go?

He was in a strange land. He knew the language fairly well. He had no particular plan. Until now, his plans could be summarized by one word, west. It did not provide for direction, detour or delay. He knew confusion well and knew how to handle it. Here in St. Pölten, under the ruins, order prevailed. A primitive order to be sure, yet it was a yardstick that applied to everyone. In a way it was reassuring. There was no war here. All the action took place east, west and north of here. He was raised in peace time. He respected borders. His reason told him the "border" was only an illusion. He knew that his present safety too was an illusion. In Germany, the safety of any young man was an illusion. Desertion of German soldiers on the western front was a wholesale affair. Many young soldiers attempted to return to their home before the end of the war. When questioned, these men usually excused themselves by saying that they were either transferred from one unit to another or simply stated that they were looking for their units, which they had been detached from through bombings and other calamities.

Hitler, in order to prevent desertion issued an order that soldiers looking for their units would be shot on the spot. The doctor could have been mistaken for a soldier.

St. Pölten was a stopover only. He knew that.

In Germany, only local traffic was permitted. A travel permit was necessary for a trip longer than twenty miles. He had to have one. Boldly he walked up to a make shift ticket window and asked for a ticket to Passau. "What can I lose?" He thought. It did not work. The young woman behind the counter explained to him that travel was restricted. Permits could be obtained at the Party Headquarters.

She was polite and charming and she smiled. Her dark uniform was well tailored and made her waist look small. She gave him directions to the Party building. He thanked her.

This was his first encounter with a German official, if one wanted to call her that. He was pleasantly surprised.

When new situations arise it is natural to compare the new with something similar in the past. He compared this obviously pretty German woman-official with some of her Hungarian counterparts, the ones he met in his travels. He was amazed. There was a tangible difference. This woman seemed to remain a person, serving him, the traveler. In peace time, in Hungary, he remembered experiencing the "don't bother me, I am busy," attitude. A picture of an "official" always busy, always unfriendly with some smart remark, and his hands ready to accept graft, reflected in his memory. He had a phobia against officials. His stomach boiled, and his fist clenched when he recalled some of his experiences.

"Germany is probably just as bad," he thought. "This woman must be an exception."

He stepped out into the street. The street names were gone, buried under rubbish and dust. Several blocks of buildings were completely destroyed. Their remains were piled high into the shape of pyramids. These, even if they guarded a dead body, did not reflect eternity. They reflected a fraction of time, in which, misery, dust, dirt, disease, and death teamed up with the heaped rubble to imitate the glorious pyramids from ancient centuries. They created a dreadful landscape that smelled heavy and foul.

The doctor followed the street and stepped over brick and plaster. German resistance was littered in the street. The buildings of organized war, planned action, and counter action were broken into small pieces. They would eventually be pulverized.

The Party building stood almost undisturbed by the war. The walls were brown stucco. The windows were clear and shiny clean. It was a two story building, massive, showing no gracefulness. A few steps led up to the heavy door. The door did not radiate welcome. It almost yelled "Keep Out!" It looked unfriendly. János felt a certain aversion, which he could not explain. It made him restless. But even with, and in spite of a negative feeling, he had no doubt that he soon would be in the possession of a "Reisegenehmigung," travel permit. His youthfulness blocked any thoughts of pessimistic color.

He opened the door that silently yielded, obviously it had been well oiled. In contrast, the war machinery was worn and rusty. Rust is a product of decay and time. Both factors plagued Germany. It has been a long time since 1938, a long time to breathe the penetrating, sometimes exhilarating, smell of gun powder. The smell penetrated coffins, cradles and standardized many odors of life. Decay was present everywhere in steel, brick, and flesh, perhaps even in some minds. Minds had to be subordinated. Minds did function in silence and silence was essential.

The hallway was clean, clear, and painted white. On the walls glorious figures of Grecian life were recreated in plaster. They imitated marble.

A young woman at the reception window greeted him. She was friendly. Her alto voice made her seem even friendlier.

He stated the reason for his visit, telling her that he had relatives near Passau. They were also refugees, he wanted to join them. She asked him some questions, which sounded like they were made out of curiosity, not official activity. She asked him where in Hungary he came from and how he managed to get this far. He asked her about his possibility of obtaining a travel permit. "Most certainly," she assured him. "Unfortunately nothing can be done today. The hour is late, everybody has left. Tomorrow morning around 10:00 AM you can get your permit."

He thanked her. He thought that everything was settled. In the morning he would have his permit. He turned around to leave.

"Do you have a place to stay?" She asked.

He could not hide his surprise. His face showed it. "No," he answered.

"You are welcome to stay at my house. In a few minutes I will be off. Why don't you just sit down? The car will be here any time soon."

He noticed the benches along the walls of the long hall for the first time. Posters looked down from the walls. There were swastikas everywhere trying to remain still and not spin. He viewed the posters with half interest.

"I am ready," she said. She stood in front of him wearing a coat made of gray uniform material. The coat was well done and was attractive.

She looked different standing there. She was more feminine, more alive. Behind the window she was part of some machinery. Now she looked like a woman.

During the past days he hardly noticed that there was a difference in sexes, not since he last saw Marika. "Where could she be?" He thought as he looked at the German woman.

She opened the door when he noticed a large poster before she turned out the lights. "On so and so March 1945, all men over 65, and youths between the ages of twelve and sixteen are to report to the Party Headquarters to serve in the Volksturm." Then the lights went out.

The date, March so and so, was to be tomorrow.

She hurried ahead to the waiting auto. She looked back smiling. It was as if she were to emphasize her obvious silhouette. He noticed that, but his taste for feminine beauty and his appetite for feminine shape had temporarily vanished. He would not come back here, he thought. That thought really was a decision. They would make him serve in the Volksturm. That was why she suggested returning here tomorrow. "Now she was offering him her home and who knows what else?" He thought. She was also offering tomorrow's insane order of being drafted into the Volksturm, a semi-military organization created in the agony of the Third Reich. He had to get out of this.

She went to the car, and a chauffer in military uniform opened the back door. She slipped in and he followed. He felt a fleeting dizziness, and registered, with surprise and certain amount of fright that he did not even try to talk his way out of the situation. On the contrary, he more or less forgot the poster and tomorrow's danger. He did not really forget, he just did not care. He was not sure what he actually felt. Perhaps it was exhaustion or maybe longing for a soft spot to recline upon, or just a desire to fall asleep, and spend a dreamless night, or a desire for a human contact filled with emotions of a child for his mother. He could not categorize his feeling. Somehow, through all of this he felt constructive. He felt slightly numb, but without coldness. For the first time since he left Szombathely he actually felt warm. He knew that it was not physical warmth. She looked at him. Her eyes were devoid of regimentation, eyes happy and promising, unlike the times.

She moved closer to him and looked at him with her large, blue, questioning eyes, "You behave strangely," she said. "You look scared. You are not scared, are you?"

"A little," he said.

She burst out laughing.

The car rolled among ruins for a while before it came to a halt in front of a massive, gray three story building.

"Here we are," she said, and picked up one of his bundles. He tried to prevent her from doing that, but she was determined. Since his German vocabulary was not elaborate but included mostly little phrases of politeness, he let her carry the smaller one of his two bundles, the one with the sugar lumps. He followed her into the building.

It was dark. No street lamps were burning. Only the moon fumbled between the clouds of spring, which were white and friendly.

They entered a large dark living room. Sure footedly she walked around the furniture and pulled down the window shades of the warm room. She switched on the lights. The lights were blinding a little. She took off her coat and threw it on an armchair. A picture of Hitler looked down upon it as it landed on the chair and sank into the velvet-plush material.

He did not exactly know what to do and less what to say. He had trouble translating his thoughts into German. It seemed to him as though flashes of phrases hurried through his brain in Hungarian, but he was unable to catch them long enough to convert them into German. He kept trying to calm his brain to the point where simple school German would catch up with it. He realized more or less for the first time in his life that human thinking took place in a language. Even emotions took place in a language. Expressions, phrases, idioms, anger, as well as joy, and anticipation took on a linguistic form in the brain before the vocal cords, fingers, or the eyes conveyed them.

He felt stiff and frozen. He felt inner warmth, but his muscles could not relax. He knew that since he was unable to express himself in German the way he desired that he must have looked rigid, an imitation of himself. "I must look awful," he thought.

He became conscious of himself. He hated that. He knew he looked bad. He was unshaven, had an haggard appearance brought about by travel and near starvation.

Altogether he did not feel great. Physically the travel affected him little. His muscles and coordination functioned well. His lips were moist and his hands and feet were warm. His face was old and red from exposure to the elements in the open trucks especially the cold night. The tense anticipation of the evening and night coming made his face more flushed. It was not that he felt different physically. Tired, yes, but that was not new or different. It was that mixed up feeling of fear of the coming events that augmented a heavy fog in his brain, which felt extensive and dense with a desire to communicate.

"Have you had lunch?" The young woman asked while she took off her dress, and put on a house coat. She did that without hesitation standing there in a slip facing him for a short second and smiling.

He did not have lunch, of course. He only had a few lumps of sugar and plenty of water.

"Let's have something to eat," she suggested. "My husband won't be home till late, perhaps after midnight."

With that she started to fix the table. The word "husband" had hit János like a shock wave of electric current. In Germany, in 1945, in the dying hours of the "Herren Rasse" a Hungarian doctor, a foreigner in the home of a married German woman without knowledge of her husband, was equal to the greatest sin in the eyes of German authorities. Fortunately their eyes did not penetrate the walls. But, when he came home and objected, "What then? What a mess?" He thought. Maybe it was all only hearsay, but he heard that the law said, foreigners who have intercourse with German women shall be executed. He was only visiting upon her invitation. What if her husband accused him?

Finally he managed to overcome his apprehension that produced nothing positive. He started to help her at the table. There was no noise outside. Occasionally a motor could be heard. Otherwise, it was quiet, extremely so for a city of this size.

It looked to him that she enjoyed the situation. She was humming a tune. The table looked nice with fine plates for two, utensils and white, ironed napkins.

"Who will win the war?" She asked suddenly. She stopped for a moment and leaning against the table with her hip. She looked at him and smiled.

He was surprised. He was convinced that all Germans were fanatic and never questioned the word of the Führer, and the Führer said Germany would win. In his mind this war was settled differently. That was the reason that he was heading west to be occupied or liberated or whatever it will be called, by the Americans. He never discussed that with any person except Marika. He had no idea that such questions were even asked in Germany. The German propaganda machine was able to penetrate the brains and the hearts of the masses with poisonous and paralyzing slogans.

She seemed sincere and was waiting for an answer.

"The side that comes up with the new invention," he answered and avoided the word "weapon." Indirectly his answer was a reference to the secret weapon promised by Göbbels.

"You are right," she said. "I know we have such an invention. We have several, as a matter of fact. Perhaps you don't know it."

She stepped to the stove and put dry wood into its belly.

"Perhaps you never heard," she continued, "of our nerve gases. They can paralyze the population of an entire city. It has a name, but I am not allowed to mention it. That is not all. Our V-2 has undergone changes and is capable of delivering the absolute weapon anywhere on this globe. Have you heard of the absolute weapon?"

"No unless you talking about the bombs that were used in Russia that killed hundreds of soldiers without ever injuring them. Entire Russian fighting units were found dead in the most unlikely position, such as sitting, leaning against trees and without evidence of injury except blood trickling from their noses and mouths."

"No," she said. "You are talking about the oxygen bomb. That is not the absolute weapon. You will see it when it is used. After the first deployment over a large city the war will come to an end. Fighting will be useless and senseless."

He did not argue or ask any questions Absolute weapon was a frightening description. He wondered, which side would use it?

She served supper, potatoes and soup. "We don't have anything else," she said. "The rations have not arrived."

She was charming. He lost most of his apprehension except one. Her husband was expected home. "What would *he* say?"

When they finished eating, she cleaned up the table and piled the dishes in the sink. Then she gave him a book, and sat down to read. Apparently she had enough conversation. János felt tired. Speaking German only was a little strenuous, so were the circumstances. The book surprised him. It was poetry by Schiller.

"A first edition of Schiller," she said and kept reading.

. "Defeat of Germany was only a few weeks away, if that long, the Russians will be here. How come she is so quiet?" He thought.

"I will make your bed," she said after a while.

"Oh," he started to say.

"Good," she remarked and hurried into a room next to the kitchen.

He was tired, his bones, his muscles, and his spirit ached. He wanted to say something more, she interrupted him by saying "Good."

"What did she mean by that?" He wondered.

She made an impression on him, a good impression, not exactly like she would have in peace time. Under different circumstances her features could be appreciated differently. His eyes would glide down from her shiny hair inch by inch across her small waist and well developed hips down to her toes. But this was 1945 a year that would end many things, ordinary things and things of beauty. Tonight in the dusty air of the war, even as glamorous as she was, even without artificial ornaments, her beauty looked distant. In these days images that the eyes picked up were not as real as what taste and touch could experience. Only what one had between his teeth or in one's fist was real. Real as long the sensation lasted. Everything else was just a mirage, just a sweet illusion before bitter disappointment.

She came back.

"Your bed is ready. Don't worry about me, just go to bed anytime you like." He was tired. She looked warm when she spoke. She looked like a mother. There is something typical about mothers. "How old can she be?" Flashed through his mind . . . "hardly more than twenty," he answered to himself.

"The bathroom is over there." She pointed to a door. "There is light in there, but the bulb is out and we are unable to replace it. Do you want me to warm some water for you?"

Most of the houses lacked central water heaters. Individual wood burning water heaters were installed in most of the bathrooms. The bath, therefore, in many instances became a Saturday night ritual. Fire wood was scarce. A large bucket of water heated on the kitchen stove and carried into the bathroom was a luxury.

"It would be great," he said. He heard the German equivalent of this Hungarian phrase somewhere. He used it now. He felt quite bold. The sentence bounced around the room, a good German sentence with a stiff Hungarian accent.

She laughed, but did not comment.

"How did the Russians behave in Hungary?" She asked suddenly. "You hear all kinds of stories, mostly bad."

"Most of the stories you heard are true," he answered.

She said, "How can the British and the Americans team up with Stalin? Unbelivable. There is only one answer. Ignorance. Don't they see that the bastions of civilization are digging their own graves when they help Russia against us? Did you know that the Russians released criminals from prisons and made them join the Red Army and told them that they would become heroes of the Soviet Union. Prisoners of war told us that."

She became emotional.

"The Party has pointed out the Russian atrocities all along. They pointed out to the world the horrible happenings at Katyn. The Anglo-Saxons are deaf. They remain consistently deaf. Why? Can you tell me why?"

"No, I can't," he said. He wanted to make some comments, but he decided not to. He was a guest here and he was in danger even without opening his mouth. He learned to limit his contribution to political discussions back in Hungary. What was said about Stalin, Hitler, Churchill, Mussolini were remembered and could be used against the commentator later on. Silence was a valuable commodity. She asked him to carry the bucket of hot water into the bathroom. He left the door slightly open to wrestle with the darkness.

"Good night," he said as he left the kitchen. She responded with a little wave of her fingers, but said nothing.

The bed was soft. A large stuffed feather bed served as a mattress and another one as a blanket. It was cold in the room, but he soon felt warm between the overstuffed feather beds.

"My grandmother used to have this kind of bed," he thought as he entered the threshold of sleep. He remembered how hot the bed felt at grandmother's during the summer, then he dozed off.

A train-scene entered his dozing brain waves with lots of people pressing against him in the small compartment. The train was moving; he was a passenger. The many bodies heated up the compartment. The conductor, a pretty, young woman checked everybody's ticket. When she came to him, she did not ask for his ticket. She smiled at him and asked "How did you like it?" He was surprised and did not answer. She asked again. The train scene faded. He felt the warmth of the bed and heard again, "How did you like it?" He opened his eyes. His young pretty hostess stood there smiling, and looking down at him in the dark room that was illuminated only by the weak light seeping through the cracked door. It was the kitchen light.

"These featherbeds came from Hungary." She said.

His head cleared.

"They feel fine," he answered. She stood there in a bathrobe, which dropped to the floor.

"This cannot be real," he thought.

He felt her body pressing against him as she got into bed. Her lips tasted fresh and her body felt firm and warm. This reality made him understand that now she was not German, not a Party member, not a mother, not a hostess, not anything else. She was simply and strictly a female, unorthodox, and different perhaps, according to his limited experience, nevertheless real, not a mirage, the real thing.

The door opened. A beam of light projected a large "V" into the room, and painted it on the floor. A man in a German uniform, János really could not tell, stood in the opening.

"My husband," she whispered and kissed him lightly.

"I will be with you in just a while. Why don't you go to bed?"

"Alright," he said.

The doctor's heart jumped and dangled from his vocal cords like a small bell sounding an alarm that he could almost hear. His throat was dry.

"Doesn't he—" he started to say.

She interrupted him. "Don't worry about him," she said, putting her head on his shoulder.

***

He woke up. Light had seeped in through the shutter. A large wall clock said five minutes to nine. A slight buzz started in his forehead behind his eyes, pulsated in both ears. It cleared rapidly as he became more alert.

He felt like stretching. He felt like going through a maneuver, which would start the flow of blood in the tiniest capillaries, and on to the cells, which meet the main stream of life. He felt like enjoying comfort for a few more minutes, but he was afraid. He heard the beating in his temples. His heart picked up speed and caused him to breathe fast and shallow. He stood next to the bed in the dark strange room when he noticed a piece paper on the night table. It was a stationary of some sort with a swastika in the left upper corner, brown paper, black ink.

He opened the shutters and held his breath to hear better when the shutters yielded without noise.

Hand written in pencil, a few lines ran across the thick paper. "I had to leave you in order to be at work promptly. I hated to wake you up, so I did not. Around ten o'clock, I will send a car for you and we will fix you up with your travel permit—Renate."

"So her name is Renate," he thought hurriedly. The clock began to chime nine. The vibration of the air had originated in the clock and had quickened his reactions. He must not remain here at ten.

The graphically perfect Volksturm posters appeared suddenly before him. "Hurry," they said. "Don't wait. Go as far as you can. You must not be drafted. Your blood must not fertilize our soil. Go away. We don't want you." His luggage lay next to his bed perplexed and wondering, the dirt and the dust from the past provided strength for the future.

"My dirty bundles," he murmured, and picked up the small one. His fingers found few more lumps of sugar. He had his breakfast. He found some water in the pitcher.

A few minutes later he was walking among the ruins in old St. Pölten heading nowhere in particular just walking away from the house where he found a few hours of rest. The place where he forgot about the war and the ruins almost completely and totally, just long enough to give his muscles more strength and his body more memories. He felt at least partially regenerated.

"Renate is her name," he thought again.

"Wonderful young woman," he murmured to himself, slightly audible to his outer ears. He continued talking to his inner perception.

"Maybe no," he said. "Who knows what motives she had? Granting a last wish?" "I bet," he mused, "she did not want me to have a travel permit. Was she even in the position of doing it? She was at the reception window. On the other hand it is unlikely," he thought. "That a receptionist would have a chauffeur driven car at her disposal, she must have had some official standing; she probably wanted me to be in the Volksturm. But then, what is the difference? And her husband, why would he tolerate her infidelity? This is outright perverted," he said loudly, then continued silently, "in bed with a strange man and the husband looking on. They both must be perverted. He must love her, Why else would he tolerate it? Does he not have any pride? He must love her. Only love can kill pride. Nothing else can."

The streets were dusty and narrow. The debris extended almost to the middle at some spots. Around the corners the heaps were high. The sun helped very little. It sent its rays bouncing around to show off the dust against the shadows. In the distance a deep rumble could be heard, far away. The sound fell from the sky. It sounded deadly as the intensity increased. The change was not sudden. In eternity, like now change occurs in a steady flow. A sudden change hardly interrupts the steady, even flow of time. This rumble was flowing evenly coming from above like waterfall. Slowly the sound gained intensity and the buildings that were still standing shook in a strange rhythm like chattering teeth. The sky was now filled not only with sounds, but with the silvery gray bodies of American bombers that slowly circled beside the fast fighter planes the Germans knew as Spitfires.

Loud flack explosions broke up this steady, grinding rumble, one after another in steady succession, smoke puffs, gray and black, first round, then disintegrating, disappeared in the sky.

Flacks were yelling, screaming, cursing and barking furiously. The planes paid no attention to them and continued undisturbed on their course. The grinding noise faded as the planes flew overhead and were gone without bombing.

He always wanted to know how the sparrows felt when the eagle flew away. Now he knew.

The ruins of St. Polten were endless like a desert. This part of the city turned into fine dust, chips of mortar and loose disengaged brick without their real color. They were bruised, black and blue. Only the smokestacks pointed skyward in the spring of 1945.

Doctor Nándor did not know what direction to take to get back to the railroad station where life in an elementary form still existed. Even now the railroad stations, while many, heavily damaged, remained symbols of freedom. They still lived in memories and in future hopes. They still served as connecting links to the rest of the world. The links to the east melted away and were gone but the west was still open. It was inviting even seducing, but only to a point. That point, perhaps, was the Rhine River. The world was shrinking for Germany. Unlike the east that was moving inward fast the movement of the armies from the west was slow east and west would meet deep inside Germany some day soon everybody expected that unless there were secret weapons as promised by Göbbels.

The doctor heard steps echoing in the ruins in all direction. He hardly noticed the time. It probably was eleven o'clock, certainly not later.

"What does Renate think now?" He asked himself. "Is she furious as a Party official should be for that foolishness even if it was pleasurable? How naïve to expect him to report back to Party Headquarters."

He left the ruins. A row of undamaged houses seemed to have defied war. There was not even a scratch, not even cracked plaster. The traffic picked up when he seemed to reach a major artery. He noticed a small sign on white background written in black ink, "Bahnhof Railroad Station." Clearly it was an improvised sign. Here he was where he arrived and started his adventure yesterday. His steps picked up.

He was hardly willing to admit to himself that the German young woman did not leave his emotions unmarked. "It was nothing positive," he murmured fully knowing that he was lying. "Just another memory." In war time, what can be moved into the ocean of memories is quite limited. Memories displace and replace each other. A symbiosis is impossible just like the Swastika and the Sickle and Hammer cannot decorate the same flag. The two flags cannot be flown next to each other because both claim the sky and one has to lose. A few hours of memory of Renate could not live peacefully with the older and better memory of Marika. They could not surround him with lovely, intelligent beauty. One had to fade. One was destined to die. At the end both died some, but it was days before doctor Nándor felt peace again, just about the time when Dönitz signed the document of unconditional surrender of Germany. When peace finally returned and was fully paid for with blood, smoke and ruins, a chunk of history was buried for ever.

"The railroad station is as busy as an ant hill," he thought.

People busied themselves carrying bundles, boxes, and luggage. One train in a disciplined attention was a contrast to the collapsed building whose roof caved to the center and was dripping with chunks of mortar as if they were stalactites. The entire skeleton of a building waved and rocked in the brisk wind that hopped and bounced from the east.

Some lively sparrows found straw and twigs in the ruins and started to build for the future. Their loud chirps had no echo because the walls were torn and the piles and rubbish were silent. No terror, no bombing, no Hitler, not even Churchill could stop the sparrows that act like their kin folk in Pittsburgh, London or Belgrade. The spring air activated the growth of new feathers, just a little brighter than the ones that served so well during the winter.

The people did not notice the birds. In their minds the ruins were talkative and more symbolic than the birds, which were the symbols of spring and love for a long time and for long eternity to come. These grave fate laden years were different. The train had an unbelievable talent and capacity to observe people, assimilate them until they were just one unit and were part of the steel complex that was about to roll west, move the magic west. The steam choked and coughed while it found its way into the dusty heavy air. More and more people were swallowed by train. The windows were open and heads filled every square inch of the opening. Eyes were searching for friends and relatives who came to say and wave good-bye. Tears glittered on worried faces. Handkerchiefs worked unceasingly, and tasted of salt, a great earmark of human emotions.

The doctor stood on the platform between two cars. His fist clenched as he held on to his bundle when he was pushed slowly inside by the oncoming people. There seemed to be no end of the crowd and the train was patient. Finally the steam turned into thunder. The whistle of the conductor got the train into a slow, lazy motion. As soon as the vibration of the moving train was felt in the compartment tensions diminished; the stiff and compressed bodies seemed to shrink a little.

Shortly, there was room for everybody to relax some, to lean, even to tilt the pelvic structure in order to rest on one leg.

The doctor found himself standing in the doorway in a small six person compartment, which now held twelve and a half people. He was the half person partially in and partially out. For some reason there was a small open spot on the luggage rack. He placed his bundles up there.

Six people were sitting down, six were standing in the middle holding on to brown leather straps hanging from the ceiling. All of the passengers in this compartment of the Italian made car were men, mostly middle aged. Only Doctor Nándor and a soldier in a Hungarian uniform were young. Nobody spoke. The air was heavy. The windows were closed and nothing kept the tired bodies from opening pores and sweat glands. The odor started to intensify.

Conversation has a basic value. It can serve in peace as well as in war time to soothe emotion. It acted like flood water running into objects, that met other waves and at the end there was calm. There was no conversation here. Emotions didn't show. They lay dormant covered by a hollow future, charred and up in smoke.

A situation like that resembled the restless state of superheated fluid that started to boil with an explosion as soon as a little vibration of a minuscule foreign body disturbed the balance of locked in power.

The hours passed without a sound generating in the compartment. It was as though everybody was concentrating on the tale of the iron wheels they spoke to the rails and the ties. They spoke of cold and misery, of torn ground, uprooted trees and families, gutted houses and people, glorious and victorious ways, and bitter defeats. They spoke of old times too. Good times, when breakfasts were leisurely and the coffee was warm, when there was music after supper and the stars did not look suspicious. Times when the blooms of the spring of everything that was rooted and leafy greeted lovers who loved not for spite, not because of power, not because of last minute desperation, but they loved for love's sake, for the sake of beauty, the beauty of their own lives and the lives of the whole world. The doctor felt the universe entering the compartment. It was there and was lingering on and on.

Suddenly a man who sat in the center of the three seated bench on the right, jumped up and with a thunderous voice and interrupted the free and mellow communication between tired minds, tired bodies, train wheels, and the universe.

"I cannot stand it anymore!" He screamed. A large black suitcase that was leaning against his knees began to shake violently as he kicked it repeatedly while he cursed in German; the meaning completely escaped the doctor.

He was tall and muscular. His hair was graying and bushy. He held his right hand in a fist and waved it around. The perplexed passengers did not dare say anything they just looked at the agitated giant. After a few deep breaths that he took through his nostrils calmness overtook him. He began to look around for a space to put his suit case that had crowded his legs.

It was bright outside but the sun hovered low in the hilly landscape. Its rays exaggerated the smoke in the compartment. There were milky waves of smoke falling and cascading, then that smoke found its way upward and exploded. The sun followed the paths of the thick smoke. Smoke stopped at the threshold of the lips where it originated and where it had disappeared. Partially because the sun's rays balanced on the doctor's bundles and partially because they presented a miserable heap, the man grabbed them and threw them to the floor where they bounced a little without a noise. Then he placed his large black suitcase on the rack. Admittedly it looked better than the doctor's bundles.

Still nobody said a word. The doctor did not feel like objecting. He considered that to be a reasonable stance. A Hungarian refugee against a German giant with German bystanders had very little chance. He quietly reached to pick up his bundles and placed them closer to where he stood. The soldier in an Hungarian uniform asked him in Hungarian, "Are these yours?"

Surprised he answered automatically.

"You damned German," the Hungarian soldier shouted. "You God damned barbarian. How dare you to touch my friend's luggage?"

"My friend," was an obvious overstatement. The doctor had never seen that Hungarian soldier before.

Later as the weeks passed and when he was secure in the American occupational zone in Germany he found that at birth every person was stamped with a mark that was recognizable by those who wore different birthmarks. The characteristics were there. Later on he was able to recognize Hungarians, Germans, Rumanians, and all other nationalities that were conglomerating in Western Germany. These were mostly displaced persons, prisoners of war, refugees of all kinds mostly from Eastern Europe. Russians were the easiest to recognize. They had an arrogant air about them, were unpolished and clumsy with watery, vacant eyes. This, of course, was an oversimplification, but he judged people by the standards that he developed by observation, he was about 90% accurate. Just by looking at the faces, just by considering the mannerisms without listening to their language such an accurate evaluation of the people was quite an accomplishment.

The Hungarian soldier must have been much ahead of him in this regard. He must have judged the German giant before he started to insult him. He must have known from his experience with foreigners how to avert a storm.

Storms have a quality of being sensational and sudden. They don't develop by the intensification of the light spring breeze. Revolutions don't develop around well developed channels. If they ever do, they are not called revolutions. To be useful, to be paralyzing, storms and revolutions lead to momentary quiet when time is suspended and the paralyzed universe weighs heavily on hearts and lungs.

After the small built Hungarian soldier finished spitting his insulting remarks in the face of the German giant, everything became unbelievably quiet. The doctor felt his heart beating in his ear drums along with the sadistic rattle of the train. The quiet was almost intolerable.

Here, in the stinking, oppressing, suffocating compartment an unbelievable thing happened. History was repeated in grossly diminished proportion, yet truly and accurately. The small Hungarian soldier dared to oppose the German giant just as the world opposed the huge German war machinery.

The tall German stood perplexed in the gloomy Italian compartment. His retaliation was much less than expected. He kept up some threatening gestures, but his answer had no quality of a sudden storm.

"Shut up you bastard," he said and waved his fist at the soldier. His large hand continued to threaten. The soldier ignored it.

"Warum riskier my leben?" (Why do I risk my life?) "So that a German swine like you can mistreat my friend?" Then switching languages he told the doctor in Hungarian, "I have diplomatic immunity. I am a courier. I must deliver important military documents from headquarters to Berlin. I have the power to arrest anyone who interferes with my travel." Then he switched to German and kept shouting.

By then everybody was participating in the discussion, if one this, pandemonium that. Everybody talked and yelled. The tall man who started it all became insignificant. Soon he was virtually ignored. The battle of words was between the soldier and everybody else in the compartment.

Meanwhile the soldier yanked the German's luggage off the rack and replaced it with the doctor's bundles. The doctor was petrified by all the noise, the tension, the near fight, and the condition of his bundles, which were about to rip any time. The bundles were taken off the rack and replaced several times, finally the doctor Nándor regained possession of them. This natural act caused emotion to settle a little and the voices became more organized. They took up the quality of discussion. After a while things became quiet.

"It must happen similarly on the front," the doctor thought. "Not only bullets, but emotions flared up. The taste for killing must become an emotional reality. He did not know. He never was a soldier."

The small Hungarian soldier was undoubtedly a brave man, foolish for sure but brave. He had experienced how to recognize and judge people. He was very resourceful and he demonstrated that a few hours later when he rendered unusual help to the doctor.

He must have had diplomatic immunity. He could not have bluffed that calmly and openly. Of course his immunity was only as good as the Germans wanted it to be. However, most Germans respected papers and documents, including papers and documents of couriers and diplomats.

The soldier had left the encircled Budapest. Two weeks previously, and made it across the Russian and German lines to the west. As he moved in a waywardly direction, so did the frontline and he was not able to slip through for two weeks. Finally, in Sopron he made it. He was going to deliver important documents from the commander of the beleaguered city. His destination was Berlin, the Führer's headquarters.

This sounded a little far fetched to the doctor. In peace time he would have hardly paid attention to such a story. In war things were different. The truth may sound fantastic. These were not times for fictional characters. Colorful and unbelievable living and functioning characters were not uncommon. The common man had the stride of a hero when he walked down the path of history that was created every hour, every minute. History was blood and flesh. At times the blood was abundant. One hundred years later, when historians indulge in so called objective research they will find only serum and water. The color will be gone.

The train began to tire some. One could feel the skipping of the wheels over the tracks. A maze of tracks was visible now. Some looked silvery; some were rusty depending on time and usage. The silver tracks were spanning the globe. They were running from Ankara to Rome, to Berlin, to Stockholm, and to many other places. Lifeline of trade, communications, pleasure, and military advances depended on the silver track. They covered vast distances of the globe. The brown neglected rusty tracks were not used. They were like clogged up arteries. They varied nourishment some time ago, but wear, changing needs, and neglect forced them to give up their role in the circulation.

The outline of a dark building emerged. The train moved closer to it in a slowly decreasing speed that eventually felt like barely creeping. With a loud clatter the train came to a halt inside the large station building.

The train arrived in Linz.

"Aussteigen," the conductor called.

"Why?"

"We will have a new train," the conductor answered. "This one will go back east immediately."

"With soldiers?"

"With Volksturm."

The doctor felt his spine tingle and get colder. His entire body shivered for a second. "Volksturm," he mumbled.

"Aussteigen," the conductor kept repeating.

His calls were drowned by the deep groans of steam escaping from the engine.

"In about two hours we will continue. We will have a new train then; it will be announced in plenty of time."

So now he was stranded in Linz. He picked up his bundle and headed toward the platform. The little soldier joined him. He carried no luggage.

"Have you got a ticket?" He asked.

"No. I just got on it in St. Polten. I haven't got a travel permit."

"They check the tickets here as the passengers leave the station," the soldier said.

"Have you traveled this way before?" János asked.

"Many times, as I said, I am a courier of the Hungarian high command. Last year I traveled between Berlin and Budapest almost every month. This will probably be my last trip. I am sure it will be. Budapest is now completely encircled. It could fall any time."

"Do the defenders expect German help?" The doctor asked.

"They are getting it from the north through Slovakia, but it amounts to nothing. It is just not enough. Not enough in materiel and not enough in moral support. The situation is desperate. When I left we still had communication with the outside but it is lost now. I am sure it is."

"How did you get through?"

"I marched at night and hid in the daytime. I was behind the Russian lines for days moving with them west. Finally, in Sopron, I slipped through."

"I came through Sopron," the doctor said.

"It was awful," the soldier continued. "All those people, all of those refugees, no place to go, just filling the streets in aimless search for shelter. It slowed down the Russians, though. Because all of those vehicles in the street they could not move their heavy machinery. That was when I slipped through their lines."

The doctor was ready to ask questions about the behavior of the Russian troops when the little soldier pointed to a small gate with a ticket booth guarded by a railroad man, and a German soldier in full battle gear.

"You go through there first and keep going. Don't look back. Just disappear in the crowd. I will catch up with you in 15 minutes over there." He pointed to a huge hall to the extreme left.

"Keep going, don't ask any questions," he said to the doctor again. He gave him a little push and Doctor Nándor entered the gate. He did not look at the railroad man, just kept going.

"Hey you!" The man shouted, "Your ticket!" The soldier lifted his head stretched his neck to spot the doctor who did as he was told. He just kept going and did not turn back. The German soldier was ready to do his duty and charge into the crowd to apprehend the doctor, but was intercepted by the little Hungarian who made it a point to block the small gate completely.

"A friend of mine," he shouted in German.

"I don't care who he is," the German answered.

"He came to see me on the train, but we had to get out. I am heading for the Führer's headquarters as soon as I get another train."

He spoke in flawless German. He still blocked the gate as the man from the railroad kept shouting, "You are blocking the exit."

"The hell with the exit," the Hungarian retorted. "He is my friend. I am telling him," he pointed at the soldier. "He is not a passenger." By this time the German soldier lost János in the crowd. Large masses of people on both sides of the gate started to get impatient. Any movement in and out was completely blocked.

Angry sounds pierced the air. "Keep going, let him go. Don't worry about the Sauhund."

The little soldier still did not think that the doctor was at a safe distance because he kept blocking the gate, and insulting the Germans.

"What did you call my friend? You swine." He was referring to "Sauhund," that was an expression often used, and was applied to anyone who was not enjoying general popularity. German prosecutors, during politically motivated trials used that expression to describe the accused.

"I risk my life for you German '*Schweine,*' and that is how you treat my friend?" The people around him did not know what this whole thing was all about, but they were insulted just the same. The crowd seldom knows; it just acts.

Finally the confusion became so great that police were called in. Three policemen arrived and quickly established the flow of humanity through the gate. They paid no attention to the two soldiers, or to anybody else. Their only purpose was to keep the gate open and flowing. They accomplished that without any difficulty. A little later the policemen retired to where they came from.

Chapter Seven

Berlin was breathing heavily. The pressure had built up to immense proportions bearable only by heroes. The population suffered. The days and the hours were counted. The resistance of Germany against the Allied pressure used up rapidly whatever time was left. The city depended only on small life lines coming from the south. These too were threatened. Their preservation was mandatory if Berlin was to be defended.

Heinrich Wolfgang Gottlieb headed for Berlin to join his family. "*Wahnsinn*" said the doctor who released him from the hospital and signed his papers. "You cannot possibly make it home to Berlin. Wait until we regain some of the lost territories."

He did not listen. He felt he could make it. He knew he could. He wanted to see his father and his little sister. His mother has been dead for years and his little sister was eighteen. He had not been home for years. It was Christmas 1941 when he spent a week of vacation at home. His mother was still alive then. A few months later she died. He did not attend the funeral because he was in Russia marching east among flowers, victory and glory.

A few months after his basic training, just a little bit after Christmas vacation, his unit was assigned to the Russian front. Germany was involved in what was to be the most impressive, most smashing *Blitzkrieg* in History. The word *Blitzkrieg* had not been used very long. Who used it first nobody knew, nobody really cared. Rapidly, by 1941, it had already become a byword like Christianity. Everybody knew the meaning.

He was heading east. The vast mountains of the Ural were his goal. It was the goal of all of the Germans. To reach a point where you can turn your back to Europe, and Asia would lie at your feet. Nizhny Novgorod was such a place. The Steppes of Asia were his goal. He represented Germany; his goal was to conquer Russia because he was young, enthusiastic, and ruthless.

It seemed so easy. The huge "pockets" and "pincers" of the Wehrmacht smashed the Russians. When Wolfgang arrived with his unit in the Ukraine the population was still in the mood of jubilation. They felt free, liberated from the Bolshevik rule. His unit arriving in the cities and villages were greeted with flowers just like the first invading troops were greeted earlier. The German political units and the secret police had not moved in yet. No oppression was evident.

Hitler's fists had not smashed hope or joy, the most desirable and most simple rights of the people.

Wolfgang was young then. His muscles were made of springs. His brain, like a sponge soaked up the impressions of the different landscapes and the different people. His Panzer unit was heading toward Rostov, the scene of what was expected to be the greatest German victory of the Russian war. In the north the front did not move. The German troops were at the gates of Moscow. The final attack was called off. The rumor had it that Moscow was to be evacuated but that Stalin would not hear of it, he stayed. In the south the German force moved rapidly toward Stalingrad.

He was a symbol of Germany but he really did not know what he was fighting for. He knew that the Russians would kill him if they could. He was in their land because he was sent there. He, like the Russians would shoot to kill. He would fight a mad, murderous and victorious war for the *Vaterland*, of course.

He was only told at school that the *Vaterland* had to be liberated. He was told that Germany suffered deep injustice after the First World War that had to be rectified. He was still in school when the war started. What beautiful school year, accelerated program; knowledge poured in then in great abundance. There were marches and rallies in support of the troops, in support of the Party and in celebration of the victories on the western front.

He did not know that the *Brandenburger Tor* stood there for another reason than to make a magnificent background for those thousands of school children and enthusiastic people who provided echo to Hitler's "*Sieg*" cries.

"*Heil*" they shouted. The Führer screamed "*Sieg.*" "*Heil*" they screamed back. All these rallies, all those well organized "spontaneous" demonstrations were magnificent. No school on rally days. Wonderful.

He did not know that Göbbels manufactured words and phrases by the hundreds if not by the thousands. He only knew that he had to learn then. He did it gladly. The *Vaterland* needed him. He knew that because Hitler, Göbbels and others told him that. He was to become a part of history. But historians did not care about him. Heinrich Wolfgang Gottlieb was not featured in history books. He had no epitaphs either. Of course he was not dead; he was very much alive in the Ukraine and now in the cold spring of 1945 as he was heading home. He was alive, but a chunk of his life was missing. His memory perhaps, maybe he was dead for a while.

He remembered the fierce battles and the blood that made the ground slippery. The taste of blood he remembered too. Taste, a little like sweat only richer. He remembered the throbbing pain in his head and his burning feet and his aching gut. He remembered all of that but he could not see the landscape. He could not activate memories of the land, of the rivers and of the sky.

He knew that a long time had elapsed between Kiev, Rostov, Budapest, and Passau. He thought that maybe these distances would remember him in the future when they try to build a future. He did not know what went on in other peoples minds, but he knew that the Poles were different, the Russians were different and some others were not. Some of his comrades matched virtually all of those he had seen in his advance and retreat. It meant that while people were different, ultimately they were all alike.

The war showed this very same thing to everybody except to the leaders. There were good people and there were bad ones. He was good. He was fair. He fought fairly and treated the enemy fairly. His entire unit was good because the commander was good.

Military units are like children, masses of people are like children. They follow the example and the influence of the commander. Some parents turn their children into animals. Some commanders commit their troops to crime and bestiality. When the top commander is insane the entire force gets dangerously close to insanity and laws are abolished. A few of the common men, in opposition, become prophets and heroes, but most reap the benefits of the digressions and they become *Mitläufer*, and accept no responsibilities. Masses do not look into the future, only individuals do.

What happened to Germany during the Hitler years could happen to civilized nations everywhere. Civilized men are taught to scrap principles for gains. The Nazi's did that on a grand scale.

Wolfgang did not know that some of his comrades turned into criminals at direct orders from above.

He did not know about the "Commissar Order." His commander ignored that document. He was a good commander.

He was thinking of theses things. The past few years allowed him very little time to think. For the first time in years, in the sick bed in the military hospital, in Passau he had a chance to reflect and to think. The more he thought, the more his desire grew stronger to get back to Berlin. He was declared unfit for further military service. He was cleared to leave the hospital. He did not ask what was wrong with him. Few patients want to know the truth. The truth is frightening.

A small column of LKWs moved slowly north in the magnificent Regental. They did not take the main road. It was too dangerous. Enemy planes were everywhere. In the comparative safety of the hills and woods they moved cautiously. They knew that the Russians were close but they had confidence that they would reach Berlin. Heinrich Wolfgang Gottlieb was a passenger in the second truck.

***

Doctor Nándor waited. People rushed and hurried. Nobody paid any attention to him. When self-preservation was the primary goal, human interest narrowed until it had no horizon at all. The doctor was on nobody's horizon. He was in nobody's field of interest. His one narrow world was a part of the total, a part of the burning globe that stood in nobody's path. He was alone. Sometimes, it is the best way to be. In 1945 it was.

There was haziness in the eyes of many men and women. Only the children's eyes gleamed. Only they could see far in the future. They ignored the days to come.

Just about seven years earlier the ancient city of Linz witnessed an event hugely different from the present misery. The houses stood proudly. There wasn't any destruction. The times were happy almost like a revolution. There wasn't any blood. There were very few tears and lots of flowers. Sixty thousand people gathered around the town hall. They were there because the spirit of the times suggested good plans were ahead. They were there to celebrate.

Years prepared them for the celebration. They were told that *Anschluss* was long overdue. When on the evening of March 12, 1938, Hitler appeared on the balcony of the town hall where nobody shouted "boo," only a small minority felt like booing. He was cheered. He was accepted. He was greeted. The crowds were influenced by the spirit of the times.

Some historians don't like to recognize that spirit!

Doctor Nándor was in Hungary then. He was in high school and was hardly aware of political happenings. He only registered the headlines, and the pictures featured in the papers. Details and backgrounds escaped him. It was okay that way. If ignorance of the present led to ignorance in the future, then it was good to be ignorant. Knowledge of the future would have made those years between 1930 and 1940 unhappy.

While he was standing in a half-way destroyed hall of the Linz *Bahnhof* he remembered the picture of the murdered body of Dolfuss. Some said that he killed himself. This event cast a shadow on the glory of the *Anschluss*. That shadow was visible as his own, and yes he followed and scanned people. He saw humped shoulders. He saw bent backs, hanging heads and hollow cheeks. He saw eyes without smiles. The people hurried, carrying all kinds of luggage to a destination unknown to him, and perhaps it was unknown to them too. Suddenly he saw the *Anschluss* as a total picture, as a continuum from the jubilation to the crumbling of the eastern front. "Without *Anschluss* the Second World War may never have occurred," he thought.

In a little while the Hungarian soldier emerged from the crowd. He was laughing. "I see you made it," he said. "Now we will try the same thing going back on the train."

"I could buy a ticket." János remarked.

"Are you crazy? Nobody can travel nowadays except with a permit."

"But all those people that got on in St. Pőlten?"

"St. Polten's different. This is Linz. This is inside Germany. There's no war here except from the sky. Just rely on me; I'll get you back on the train."

The crowd filled the huge main hall of the station to capacity. For the first time, as he looked around, he noticed large signs covering the battered walls. The bombing broke the windows, caused plaster to peel off but the structure stood solidly, or at least that was the assumption. Huge posters greeted the travelers.

" *Feind hőrt mit.* "

"*We capitulieren nie.*"

The doctor was surprised to see the signs. In his eyes the enemy existed in the frontlines and in the occupied territories. In those areas that were "liberated" as the enemy would say. Now he was confronted with reality, the enemy within. He was disappointed. Somehow through all these blood drenched years he thought that the fight was fair, men against men, machine against machine, economy and materiel against the same on the other side. Now he realized that it was not so.

While looking at the signs almost instantly, years of experience marched in front of his eyes. Time, shape and color suddenly appeared like reality. The little Hungarian soldier standing beside him became a familiar person. He looked like another little soldier in his home town in Hungary guarding an American flyer, a tall man, young, and blond like the Germans . . . he was a prisoner of war, a casualty figure, one of the thousands. It did not occur to him that the American could have been a paratrooper, not just a pilot shot down. In that case he could have had helpers. Your neighbor could be a *feind*, or even a friend. The main threats to security were not foreign spies, but the saboteurs, dissenters, the *"verräter."* He now understood that in Germany, in Hitler's Super Germany that kind of problem existed, although officially only one group of people enjoyed full recognition, the heroes.

"Do you have anything to eat?" The soldier asked.

"Lumps of sugar." He gave him a few.

"Sugar, a great food to have," the soldier said.

"I saved over the months."

"Hope we will get our train soon."

The train was on everybody's mind. Would it come? Would all these people be stranded? Everybody knew that someday, probably soon everybody would be stranded somewhere. It could be a factory, a railroad station, a church, or perhaps a coffin on the way to the cemetery, but inevitably every person would be left alone to himself. Even the past would disappear. There would be no shadow, no contrast, nothing would be bright, and nothing dark, just gray and meaningless gray. The people knew that the day would come when defeat would stop everything that is in progress now. It would reroute paths. It would stop the rivers from flowing. It would make its mark on everybody's life. People did not know that the defeat would have its blessings, not the way the victor's hoped. All the allied plans, if indeed there were reasonably detailed plans, amounted to nothing as compared to the deep and effective liberation of the population from their past both immediate and ancient.

One of the most magnificent feelings is the loss of everything. Against these feelings ordinances and laws are written. Against these feelings millions of people had been fighting everyday in civilized countries. Only profiteers, saints and madmen know this feeling. This feeling was inaccessible to others. Now very soon in a big, beautiful, thunderous blow, the allied forces were ready to give one of the greatest feelings to the hated enemy. The German people and their allies did not dream how great the taste of defeat was. It was like a religious experience, indescribable, alien to the brain, property only of the heart. Doctor Nándor did not know that. Vaguely he felt that happiness was not far. Unconsciously he recited the words of the great Hungarian poet, Endre Ady, "Happy are those who start again and again."

Many never start again. The dead will not rise again. Yet, there is no blood lost in vain. Every drop of blood purified the past and every drop of blood made a mark on somebody's life. The red rivers of blood surging at times like spring water made their mark upon the universe. After 1945 no part of life could be the same. The earth, the stars, millions of people, the constellations, the galaxies, would have to change to guarantee sanity for the future. For blood must not see sunlight. Blood may not mix with dirt and dust, without changing the image of God. He who gives his life changes other's lives. This has always been the earth's law from Abel and Christ to the millions that died during this war. Spilled blood saves the lives of those who are left, whether they admit it or not.

"It is time to go back to the train," the little soldier said. He grinned a little. At this point the doctor noticed the movement of the crowd that like one unit compressed to get closer to the control booth. Some started to pass. The doctor felt uncomfortable. His throat began to throb and his feet felt weak as they approached the booth. The guard has been changed. A very young pale looking soldier stood there and leaned against the booth. He paid little attention to people.

"Don't you worry," the little soldier said. "Just keep going like before. Get on the train while I hold their attention."

"Where do I meet you?"

"I'll find you."

The recent scene of sharp exchanges of words between the ticket clerk, the German guard, and the Hungarian soldier intensely repeated itself. Almost instantly the doctor was lost in the crowd. He was able to enter the train. He hurried like the other people. He did not even look back from the platform.

In a half hour or so the train started to jerk and with painful stretching of its body began moving toward Passau. The little soldier and doctor Nándor stood at a window motionless, without a word. Their eyes followed the smooth body of the Danube River. The water looked brownish gray not blue.

"Perhaps there were days when the Danube *was* blue," the doctor thought. "Strauss must have seen the river when it was blue."

His thoughts jumped from one thing to another, from the present to the past. It felt to him as if his thoughts merged with universal consciousness and became part of everything else. He felt the thoughts and emotions of all the other people. Centuries expressed themselves in plain view and many things in the past world became exquisitely clear. It was beautiful, frighteningly so. Beauty was frightening sometimes. His heart caused throbbing pressure in his temples. He had never had an experience like this before. He had never felt this close to universal truth. He had never felt extraordinary visionary qualities before.

He felt an irrepressible urge to express all of this clearly, put it down on paper, but he realized just as he accomplished that goal the picture would disappear, and he'd loose his connection to universal consciousness. He became deeply depressed. He stood at the window almost in a trance. Slowly the landscape emerged again like in a normal day.

"How will this all end?" The soldier asked.

"Evil will triumph," the doctor answered.

"What evil?"

"I don't know."

"We have seen enough evil already," the soldier remarked and gazed into the distance. "We have seen enough destruction and too many people are dead."

"The dead are harmless; the living are evil."

"Maybe, but not every one of them, I knew a young woman, she was good, perhaps the only living thing good to me."

The soldier paused a little and continued. "I have not thought of this that way until now. Now that you say it, it seems clear. People are bad, awfully bad, but she was good."

"Tell me about her," the doctor suggested.

"What's the use, she's dead now."

"I am sorry."

"She was killed, raped and killed."

"The Russians?" The doctor asked.

The soldier nodded. Tears filled his eyes, but they tried not to run down his cheeks. They found their way to the inside, into his throat. He said nothing more. Doctor Nándor left him with his thoughts. Everybody must have a chance to be alone with his thoughts at times. For the little soldier this was the time.

Later, the soldier asked, "Don't you think war is suicide?"

"I do very much so, sanctioned, calculated, suicide."

"Maybe you don't understand. I don't mean murder. I don't mean that war legalizes murder. I mean that this whole business of war is suicidal. The leaders have a desire to commit suicide. But they are cowards. That is why they send others to be slaughtered."

The doctor knew exactly what he meant. Killing is only a front, a cover up.

The train was moving west at a steady, comfortable pace. It was the pace of safety. Passau was not far away.

***

The train pulled slowly across the line that used to be the border between Bavaria and Austria. A little while later it stopped in Passau.

1945 / Joseph J. Kozma

The air rested peacefully around the buildings. Few military vehicles could be seen. The people looked like they would in peace time. They weren't in any particular hurry. Women chatted at street corners. Children played in the yards. People breathed slowly and evenly. In contrast, the travelers who just had arrived from Linz looked torn and patched, like the resurrected dead. Resurrection does not mean glory, not in a war of continents.

The railroad station was clean. The aisles were swept and washed. In the middle of a large, concrete aisle, under the deeply vibrating sky, a large group of people was having a feast of some sort. They were conglomerating around large aluminum pots that seemed to contain some type of food steaming and sending out tantalizing aromas. Men, women, and children, were holding cups in their hands, and their lips eagerly slurped a grayish liquid. The doctor and the soldier approached the group and identified a Red Cross sign next to another poster that announced that "Free Soup" was available.

This soup combined vegetables and water and was available for free. It was the most elementary of foods. And, the most wonderful result of fire and water. The two universal extremes bubbled in big pots with a delightful aroma, which appealed to the hungry masses.

Dr. Nándor enjoyed a cup of hot soup. It contained bits and pieces of vegetables, barley kernels and a few woody pieces of undetermined nature, perhaps oats or rye with sharp cutting edges. That was the first warm food he'd had in days except for the soup in Renate's home. The Red Cross workers prepared the free soup as an act of kindness on behalf of others, for their preservation, and not only for themselves.

The soup tasted good, not like anything he ever tasted before, not, like the carefully blended stew his mother used to make, and not even like the "secret recipes" of some of the fine restaurants he used to know. This soup was not for culinary pleasure, not for connoisseurs to smack their lips over. This clear broth liquid was prepared to give their sluggish, weary blood some speed. It was cooked for one purpose, to give life; it was made to preserve life.

The doctor and the soldier sat down on a bench. They ate the hot soup. Some dried leaves that survived the winter fell on the meticulously clean concrete. They were chasing each other in ever shrinking circles. Then, after touching each other for a fraction of a second they flew apart to start the game again. "Just like lovers," the doctor said.

"What?" The soldier asked.

"Those leaves are just like lovers," the doctor responded. "See how they are attracted. See the vibration of their frail bodies. See their embrace. See how they start over like lovers?"

The leaves continued their dance over and over.

"Just how long can happiness last like that?" The doctor asked without moving his lips.

Time mercilessly pounded inside their ears with every heart beat. One can tell time by their own heartbeat. In war the heart becomes an important timepiece. And then the time came for the little soldier to continue his journey toward Berlin.

"I probably will not make it," he said. They shook hands. For a chapter of their life was closing a chapter of short fused emotion. With the sharing of sugar and soup, theirs had been a warm friendship.

***

Heinrich Wolfgang Gottlieb jumped out of the truck as the column halted suddenly. Soldiers and civilians emerged from the other vehicles.

"*Was iist los?*" Everybody shouted. A shell burst violently among the vehicles. The dirt, smoke and debris flew in straight lines creating a picture of an immense black flower that enveloped the trucks, the people, and the landscape. Another explosion followed, then another, and another. Then it became quiet. Only the wounded and the dying moved. The spared and the dead lay still as close to the ground as if they were one unit.

"The Russians," somebody shouted.

Ahead, at a distance measured by fear rather than in meters the large gray mass of a steel monster with a red star blocked the road. A Soviet tank was pointing its cannon at them.

Everybody who was not badly hurt scattered to the roadside. Bent backs and folded knees rapidly disappeared behind rocks, bushes, and trees.

Wolfgang was covered with dirt. For a fraction of a second he felt dizzy and for a much smaller fraction of time, measured only by his heart beat, he felt paralyzed. Then he felt his head filling with warmth and his face with color. His arms and hands came to life first as he pushed himself up. Then his legs returned to full function. Gradually he freed himself from dirt and oil that covered him. Next to him his truck lay turned over. Ahead of him his driver rested on his back his eyes fixed to the gray haven, his chest cut open by the blast. His blood looked black mixed with dirt. A few drops of red blood trickled from his mouth.

The tank moved closer. The grinding rattle of the motor surged through Wolfgang's brain; he had to survive. More than that, he had to destroy. He had to fight the tank. He felt a great chance unfolding in front of him. He felt a compulsion to fight. He felt more than a duty now. The *Vaterland* was dead anyway. Not for the *Vaterland*, not for his people, only for himself, he had to fight. Not capitulate, but fight or die.

He took cover.

Shots, deep rolling shots could be heard at a distance. The double thuds of the "*Panzefausts*" told him the story. The Russian tanks were brought to a halt. To his right he saw T34's either standing or moving very slowly. He could not see the German positions. The one tank blocking the road and coming toward them was completely separated from the rest. No ground troops followed it.

The Russians must have intended to get as far west as possible. This must have been an advanced unit. Wolfgang's truck crossed the Elbe at Riese a few hours earlier. They were told that the road to Berlin would be safe. Apparently it was not. He knew he had to make it, but first he had to fight, and had to win. The tank came closer. The abandoned trucks trembled on the road.

He ran under the trees. For a few seconds he stopped. His chest heaved. His hands felt hot and moist. Taking cover behind every tree and every bush he began to run to the end of the column of trucks. One of the trucks, though he did not know, contained weapons. What kind of weapons he also did not know?

"Anything will do," he thought, "a grenade, a pistol, a knife, anything." He had no doubts that he would win. The road curved, he lost sight of the truck. He ran on the road now.

"*Was ist passiert?*" Somebody at the end of the columns shouted.

"*Die Russen.*"

Three or four soldiers were busy unlatching the canvas cover of one of the trucks. Wolfgang jumped up onto the running board, and then into the truck bed. Cannon fire could be heard. The rattle of the lonely tank grew louder.

"*Wolfgang du brauchst nicht zu kämpfen.*"

"*Verdammt,*" Wolfgang answered. "Give me that *Panzerfaust.*"

He picked up the bazooka, the only one in the truck. The sight of a case of anti-tank grenades gave his body extra strength.

"Hurry up!" He shouted. "Let's get behind a tree. You load me; I'll fire." The young soldier he addressed followed him. The others scattered with whatever weapons they took from the truck.

Wolfgang lifted the bazooka up on his shoulder.

"Load," he said. The young boy in soldier's uniform hesitated. "I don't know how," he shook his head.

Wolfgang felt like laughing, laughing at the war and at the world.

"Where did you get your training?"

"In Wűrtzburg."

"Look, this is how you do it."

The bazooka was loaded. The right index finger was on the trigger. The tank appeared around the bend and shoved some of the trucks off the road.

Wolfgang stared at the large steel body. He focused on the upper front of the tank. He waited then he pulled the trigger. A black hole yawned where the explosion hit. A fire burst toward the sky, thick black smoke spread around the trucks and into the trees. No sign of life came from the wrecked monster. Wolfgang fired once more. Pieces of steel scattered and followed the smoke.

Suddenly, the passengers who took cover among the trees of the small forest ran electrified back to the road.

Wolfgang, his right shoulder sagging, carried the bazooka and climbed up on a small hill and took cover behind a tree. He was able to look down on a large grassy meadow. He saw burned out machinery but no other activity.

Jubilant passengers ignored the dead and congratulated him. There was jubilation. Somehow everybody forgot the possibility of danger ahead. In war every moment has its own meaning, great opposites can alternate in rapid order.

Wolfgang smiled but, internally, he noticed an unexplainable feeling. He suddenly saw missing episodes coming alive from his immediate past. He now remembered the long road from Stalingrad to Passau. This small victory reminded him of the inevitable defeat. He sat down on a rock next to the road. He buried his head into his palm. They smelled like oil and smoke.

Germany was lost. He knew that the same Germany would never return to life. Smoked out guts of destroyed tanks would guarantee that. He remembered now the battle for Budapest. The fierce street fights came to him vividly. The images of his comrades marched in front of him. He saw Hungarian soldiers and civilians even children moving from the shelter of one house to another carrying what was to be known as Molotov cocktails. They all fought with him.

He remembered the huge trench, which spanned the flat land between the Danube and the "Blond River" Tisza. It started on the western side south of Budapest, and ran to the east to the river that according folklore, or history perhaps was sheltering the body of Attila the Hun in caskets of gold, silver, and iron. After some 1,500 years after the body of the Hun was put to rest, and his pall bearers were put to death. This area received floods of Hungarian, German, and Russian, blood.

He remembered another tank in Budapest, another T34. It moved slowly like this one. It rolled slowly toward him. It was raining. The raindrops were cold, some were frozen. The ground was soft on the surface. The mud was ankle deep. Deeper, winter still was holding on. He lay on the ground. He had no cover. Around him lay scores of dead. He pretended to be one of them. His right hand clinched a canteen filled with gasoline. A piece of cloth torn from his uniform was squeezed into the neck to serve as a wick.

The ground shook violently. He could hear the ground scream in pain as the T34 marred the surface. His left arm was stretched out. His right arm was buried in the mud. It was under his body hiding the canteen. His legs were apart with his right knee bent. He looked like the dead that were around him.

He saw mud splatter around him. The tank moved closer. It was heading toward the left arm. He saw the great steel mass as it crushed a body into the ground.

He waited. His throat throbbed as he held his breath. His skin was chilling. He felt paralyzed. It was the same kind of paralysis that he felt just a few minutes ago. As he felt that way he thought that paralysis must be the beginning of an action. He closed his eyes. The tank came closer. He felt his paralysis disappear. The tank was just a few feet from him. He pulled up his right hand. His right knee pushed him up out of the mud. He crouched next to the Russian monster. He knew that he was out of sight of the gunners. The intended victim gave him cover. He lit the match. The wick hungrily picked up the tiny flame and magnified it many times. He stood up and jumped into the air. Now was the moment. He could not fail now. The hatch of the tank was open. He had to aim accurately. His arm took a swing with the canteen and its fiery tail. It was up to fate now. He returned to the mud. He did not remember how long he lay there. One heart beat, two and more, nothing happened. His brain worked violently. What was wrong? Why was there not an explosion? The Vaterland must be protected. Why was there silence? To him anything other than an explosion meant silence. Four more heartbeats, then five, finally the ground shook and burning oil splattered. The tank stopped. Smoke escaped into the air. He did not move. Ten more heart beats. There wasn't any sign of life from the tank. He jumped up and shouted, "I got him . . . I got him . . . see, I got him." He jumped up and down like he was possessed. He skipped and hopped in a circle talking to those who were approaching him. "See, I did it, he's dead," he pointed to the tank. As he turned round there was nobody, but the dead. It became clear to him that in the elation of victory he had hallucinations. He saw his dead comrades alive because he needed witnesses. A hero need witnesses, otherwise he was nobody.

After the vision of the gathering soldiers faded he saw miles and miles of devastation. Guns, helmets, and bodies were scattered not in a pattern, but by the cruel calm of chance. Death has no pattern. In war it does not give you a choice. It throws you in a big chaos and kills you at random. At random you fall, at random you die. As he looked around and saw the dead all around him, he wondered how he could be alive. He was very much alive and wanted to make a report. He wanted to be recognized. He did what was expected of him. When a day later, hungry and weak he reported the tank incident at headquarters, they laughed at him.

"Du spinst," the captain said. "Where are your witnesses?"

"They are dead."

"Dead witnesses," the captain shook his head and dismissed him.

From that point on, he did not remember anything. He was told at the hospital that he was picked up in Szombathely and transported to Passau. In the hospital bed, while lying there with his eyes closed and motionless he heard the doctor in charge saying, "War does not only produce dead and heroes, we have in-betweens. Heinrich cannot face this fact." He called him Heinrich. He did not know that his father called him Wolfgang.

"The doctor was right in a way," he thought as he sat there with his face buried in his hands. "But he was wrong too."

He was no in-between. He was a hero. He was a hero, but had no proof then. This time he had proof. He had witnesses, he had proof, but he had to prove to himself that indeed he acted just a little past bravery, just a little detached. He felt lonely. The brave still have company, but heroes are alone. Their friend is the Universe. He remembered the vision that he saw in the hospital in Passau. Suddenly he saw the white deer again. He shrugged his shoulders, stood up slowly, and tossed his bazooka into the woods. "You did a good job," he shouted. "Goodbye."

There was silence now. The war went on silently, but the smell of oil and fire kept on lingering.

Most everybody climbed up on the highest hill to gaze down to where the battle was still going on. Many tanks were still and smoking, many others were retreating to the east.

In a few minutes a bicycle unit of the so called destroying division that was created by the order of Hitler on January 26th, rolled among the vehicles.

"*Was ist los?*" The lieutenant shouted.

The excited men informed him about the destruction of the advanced Russian tank.

"What is you name?" The lieutenant asked Wolfgang. He made a note in his book. He put down Wolfgang's serial number and some more information that he gathered from the other soldiers.

He shook Wolfgang's hand. "I recommend that you receive the Iron Cross immediately, present this paper to my headquarters in Berlin. Heil Hitler!"

***

Doctor Nándor looked after the vanishing figure of the little soldier. Long after he disappeared from sight he kept gazing in the direction of the departure. They only spent a few hours of travel together, but these hours seemed fateful and significant. The soldier helped him to get this far. Without his help he probably would be in Linz, or perhaps be retained like so many unauthorized travelers. He had a warm feeling of affection for the soldier who acted like a devoted friend.

"A friend for a few hours," he murmured. "Friend forever if I see him again." He continued, "I hope he makes it."

He was in Passau. Where from here? How and where stood the war now? How far was the western front? There was no reliable way to find out. The German account of the war embellished with rosy colors of secret weapons, and ultimate victory even though fierce fights were taking place on German soil. The heart of Germany was bleeding. Exsanguination "bleeding to death" was only a question of time.

He noticed a great number of Hungarians, mostly members of the *Nyilas Party,* displaying the red, white and green armbands with the crossed arrows, the Hungarian swastika. They seemed to move about freely and were in an upbeat mood. Their excellent clothes were in contrast to the attire of the Germans, and of that of the refuges of recent arrival. The doctor learned that large numbers of Party officials and members of privileged classes were evacuated from Hungary some weeks ago in comparative comfort. These people were able to bring much of their valuables with them, which they displayed in shameless arrogance to the dislike of the Bavarian population.

The Party set up something like a headquarters in Pfarrkirchen just a little to the south. Bavaria became a stronghold of the Hungarian Nazi movement. It was assumed that the Szálasi cabinet was somewhere nearby working on plans for ultimate victory.

There are people who are chronically optimistic. They always hope and usually lose. Hope and hard work are seldom in each other's company. Hopes and dreams, work and solid realism make more impressive teammates. Hopes and dreams were the Hungarian's mental and emotional makeup now. They thought that somewhere somebody was trying feverishly to defeat the Russians. Many Germans felt the same way. When defeat was discussed among the Germans or among the Hungarians it concerned only the Russians. They did not really care if the Western Allies were the winners. They feared only the Russians. The news coming from the Russian occupied territories described looting, murders, and rape.

At this point nobody in the German camp was fighting for victory. A very few military leaders considered the perpetuation of the war, a war without end, a war without defeat, and without victory. The population did not know that the leaders were preparing for the end. Their faces did not show it, but there was a general feeling of doom. There was a feeling that occupation by the Western Allies would not be bad at all.

A big uncomfortable shadow disturbed their dreams. The waiting hours brought thoughts after thoughts of what the defeat might taste like and what could be done to erase the bitterness. Sober judgment dictated that the western influence should be extended as far east as possible. Since the population had absolutely nothing to say concerning the events to come, they kept on dreaming in the daytime and hoped that Americans, British and French would be their occupying masters. Even in defeat most people felt secure and protected in the west.

Trains came and trains left. The free soup kitchen never stopped working. The pots never seemed empty. The doctor felt more relaxed. His nagging stomach felt calmer now. The warm soup had a nice soothing influence. He walked back into the station. There was a peace time atmosphere inside. The station was clean. The departures and arrivals were clearly posted. The ticket windows were in full operation. He decided to take a chance like he did in St. Pőlten. Suddenly he recalled the picture of a German girl, and as that entered his brain it affected his emotions too, a little.

"Marika was a warm young woman. Warmth is badly needed in this miserable spring," he said to himself in the inner language that he used frequently during his travel.

To his amazement nothing drastic happened. Without question and without hesitation he was given a ticket to Pfarrkirchen. He paid a ridiculously small sum, and that was that. He entered the train in an uplifted mood.

Inside the train he found the atmosphere much different from what he had experienced in his travel. The train obviously carried local travelers, shoppers, and visitors, not refugees not anxiously fleeing, and running individuals. These travelers were well fed, contented people who were living by their habits and schedules and loved it.

The train wheels did not scream and squeak. They did not make noises of fear and breaking bones. These wheels played a rhythmic, familiar music, like a lullaby. The engine spit its smoke proudly that relaxed high in the sky. This train was like new, never threatened by death, not yet, not now. Tomorrow might bring disaster, but until then the present day stays alive. If everything goes right, tomorrow will be another day. So, life goes on until it goes out then there is nothing.

The landscape was gentle. The hills rolled gaily and smoothly like in a story book. The train whistled in a carefree manner. Doctor Nándor enjoyed the ride. The frequent stops were gentle. They were different from all of his previous train rides with humanity shoulder-to-shoulder packed solidly, heat exchanging freely from body-to-body. These eyes of passengers were different. They almost smiled. Some people sang, not songs of war, not marches, but songs of life, and songs of yesterday. Everybody was seated, nobody had to stand.

Du, Du liegst mir im Herzen,
Du, Du liegst mir im Sin;
Du, Du machst mir viel Schmerzen,
Weisst nicht wie gut ich dir bin.
Ja, Ja, Ja, Ja,
Weisst nicht wie gut ich dir bin.

The song went on. It never seemed to end. Ja, ja, ja, ja . . . came over, and over again, and became louder, much louder as everybody joined. The song was easy to follow, and in a little while, the doctor hummed along. Without words, without a fixed meaning, just in its rhythm and melody the doctor joined in. And then somebody started another song, "*Trink, trink, Brüderlein trink.*"

A few others chimed in, and in a short while the two songs competed with each other until everybody shouted, and finally broke into hysterical laughter. It was a nice train ride.

After a little while, like so many times during his journey the doctor was lost in his memories. He remembered the train trips he made as a child across the hills of his homeland, across the golden fields of wheat, which were adorned by millions of blood-red poppies. The vibrant red fields of poppy blossoms, the white, pink, and purple mixture of the cultivated poppies and the literally millions of bachelors buttons made the Hungarian countryside an unbelievable and unforgettable experience. From this distance, from the Bavarian late winter in the year 1945, with the colors of gray, black, and red only due to blood, the train rides of his youth appeared like a dream.

As a child, he accepted the unbelievably beautiful contrast nature provided for man to enjoy all over the Hungarian landscape as something natural, something that could not be any other way. For children believing was a simple thing, as simple as breathing, as simple as dreaming. It was the adult mind, even the adult emotion that needed proof, proof of everything even proof of existence. How else could Descartes state, "*Cogito, ergo sum.*" That this statement had ever to be made was infinitely sad, that the question whether one exists or not was raised at all was even sadder. Because when you don't believe a kiss, when you toss joy into the mud, when you trample anything that scorns, frowns, sobs, smiles, giggles, shouts with fear, or with wild elation, you indeed will need proof that you are alive. Your brain will give you that proof, but only the proof that was half of you. Many people are satisfied with the provable half. But, if you couldn't see that the square root of minus one was an irrational number, or if you don't appreciate the fact that you cannot cry when you concentrate on observing yourself, then you lose the half of yourself, the one half that uses the act of thinking for proof. There were two halves, one thought, the other felt, and together they made *you* whole, made *you* great.

"*Pfarrkirchen*," the conductor shouted. A neat little station, clean without war damages greeted the passengers. The evening whispered into their ears a little colder than expected the street lights weren't burning and there wasn't illumination of any kind.

"Don't use lights. We are under warning. There could be an air raid any time," somebody declared in the foggy darkness. "This way everybody." Here and there a burning cigarette showed the way. Everybody moved in silence. Their happy songs died on their lips. If those songs lived in their hearts, there was no way to know.

The doctor had no place to go. In a way he was satisfied to be as far as *Pfarrkirchen*. He even considered vaguely settling here temporarily and waiting it out, so to speak. Before he left Hungary he heard that some of his acquaintances were in Peterskirchen II. According to his map it wasn't very far from here. He thought he might want to try to get there tomorrow. There was very little to do tonight. He needed a place to stay. So, he decided to break from the silent crowd and slipped quietly into one of the trains that was yawning on one of the side tracks. He thought that he would spend a lonely night. He was surprised to see that other people had the same idea. The train was packed. It was hard to find a bench to sit down. He moved from coach to coach, stepped over legs and luggage. His bundles were in his way too. He found it hard to squeeze through the narrow passageways that were cluttered with luggage and sleeper's legs.

Finally, he came upon an empty bench and took possession of it. It felt good. It felt wonderful to stretch out on the shiny, wooden seat. His head felt heavy, and he slowly let his body tilt sideways, until his head touched the bench. He, automatically, pulled up his knees and swung them up on the cold varnished planks. He lay on his side. His face felt the coldness of the unheated train. A few minutes later sleep wrapped its protective blanket around him, and sheltered him from the world.

The morning brought sunshine, grief and outrage to *Pfarrkirchen*. A small boy was killed by aircraft gunfire, by what was assumed, an American. The boy was hit from a low flying aircraft when he was with his father in their milk truck with shiny milk cans. The first timid rays of the sun bounced off the cans and showed them off to the wide blue sky. When the plane came, the machine gun barked. Milk found its way to the ground where the boy lay killed by bullets. The Germans called it American gangsterism. Murder they called it, brutal gangland murder.

That gasoline has been concealed and transported in milk cans in some other parts of the country during this dirty and sometimes heroic war nobody seemed to know about, or pretended not to know. Nobody thought that the flier could have mistaken the milk truck for ammunition supply truck. Nobody dared to consider it. If you got killed your killer was a gangster. If you kill you are a hero. So was the taste of the war. So was the taste in 1945.

Upon awakening, the doctor felt stiff and aching in his body, clear and confident in his head. Sleep gives confidence. It recharges the cells so that they may function again as they meant to function at the time of the Genesis. During sleep the cells return to omniscience. A rested mind comprehends the universe.

The doctor stretched and felt that he comprehended the war. Suddenly his thoughts were interrupted by a vision, or perhaps by his imagination. As he looked, out of the train window he spotted Marika as she hurried along with the other travelers. Here in *Pfarrkirchen* the picture of the little girl that he got in the confusion of leaving Hungary popped up. Was it just a vision? She looked real. Apparently she took the same road, the same path. Why had he not sensed it before? Living creatures make an impression around them as they take and change their space in the universe. These impressions can be picked up and decoded by others. It is love that can reconstruct the fragments the best; it can pick up the vibrations that ride on the winds; it can find the missing stars; it can put together a living image. "Was that happening to him?" He wondered.

He never expected to see her here. He grabbed his bags and hurried to get off the train. He kept watching her through the windows, but by the time she reached the platform he lost her. She was in a crowd that was boarding another train. He hopped across tracks to reach the hurrying people. A railroad man of some sort hollered at him with little enthusiasm. He did not pay attention to the man and he did not insist. There was none of the hectic rush here that he experienced in Linz when the soldier got into argument with the official. Here people hurried not out of fear, not out of lack of time, but out of cold *Pűnklichkeit*, out of desire to be on time.

Marika was nowhere to be seen.

The train steamed slowly out of the station. She must have boarded it. He looked after the train with clenched fist. He wanted to curse but he did not.

At least she was here. She did not have luggage. She must have been located here. Now that they were both here he felt a divided emotion; he was glad and he also had a feeling of let down. He could not explain it. He felt as if he had arrived. He could stop running. He could wait for the end of the war here. If the Russians should occupy this area he still could go farther west. Marika would be with him then.

A sudden thought entered his mind. Maybe somebody brought her to the station, perhaps her father. He hurried out of the building. There were many people in front of the building, not exactly a crowd. Vehicles were lined up, horse pulled wagons, and horsepower loaded trucks, and cars formed a neat unit.

A voice, vaguely familiar greeted him. It was not an annoying voice. It called his name, "János . . . Doctor Nándor?" It was Marika's mother. She looked great. She was dressed elegantly in a sport suit and drove a carriage with a beautiful pair of horses.

"When did you get here?" She asked

"Just last night. How wonderful to see you. You must have left Szombathely in a hurry. I hoped that I would catch up with you some place, in Sopron, perhaps."

"We came through Kőszeg. It seemed closer. Did you come through Sopron?"

"Yes."

"I hear there was a terrible bombing there. Hundreds died on the square where all the cars and wagons were jammed."

"If there was a bombing it must have been terrible, all those people, and hundreds of vehicles, and not an inch of unoccupied space. When I came through the traffic had not moved for eight hours."

"And the people were just waiting?" She asked.

"Waiting and waiting with hope and patience."

"I would not have," she said. "I would have left everything and walked."

"That is what I did."

"You lost everything?" She cried out with astonishment and indignation. She sounded as if she just heard something truly terrible. It was a mixture of pity and joy. Many Hungarians changed the pitch of their voice in those days just like she did. Hearing it, he experienced a different kind of feeling. A feeling of support and sympathy, many refugees experienced the same feeling, a feeling of suffering and relief in one emotional package. It was fashionable to suffer in those days. The people talked about their own losses and the losses of others. Their voices carried that same tone in 1945.

"I did not have much to begin with," he said.

"Is this all you have?" She pointed to his bundles.

"Yes."

The bundles looked miserable contrasted with her. She looked as if she had just emerged from the dressing room of her country estate. She wore gloves and a hat. They looked strictly out of place. In general, nobody paid much attention to their attires. People wore what they had. She was in a foreign land, but showed off as if at home in Debrecen.

Because of their clothing that they salvaged the refugees looked different in Szombathely too. But the contrast was more pronounced here, in a foreign land. They looked fancy and show offish. Some behaved stupid to say the least. That made things worse.

"Where did you stay last night?"

"In one of the trains."

"Then you haven't settled yet. Will you stay here or keep going?"

"I will stay."

He was still standing next to the carriage. She looked down on him. That made him uncomfortable.

"Which way will the Americans go? Will they go north to Berlin, or this way?" She asked.

He had no idea. Nobody did. It was the general opinion that the Allied Headquarters did not know it either. Eisenhower has not made a decision. But soon it was decided that Berlin would be for the Russians to take and that the American troops would move across southern Germany and into Bohemia.

"This way, I hope," the doctor said.

"Listen János," she started bending over and in a tone of intrigue and secrecy she continued. "Come with me to our Lager. We have got about thirty people there. We have room for one more."

"I hardly can impose upon you."

"Don't talk foolish, János. Marika will be happy to see you."

"Did I see Marika here at the station?"

"Yes she was going to Eggenfelden. She will be back this afternoon. It is only a stone's throw away. Well, are you coming?"

He got into the carriage. It was shiny black. The front seat was plush velvet. There was some gold trim too. It was an elegant vehicle, obviously brought over from Hungary.

"We came in this thing," she pointed to the carriage. "It is the most practical way to travel. It is light and roomy. The horses don't get exhausted."

"You mean you came all the way from home in this carriage?"

"Yes, and no," she answered. "We started out driving west. We caught up with a train transporting some materiel to the west. It was a freight train and even had a few empty cars. We loaded the whole thing on the train, horses and all, and here we are."

"Wonderful," he answered. "You're looking fine."

"Thank you, János."

"How is Marika?" He asked.

"She's fine. You'll see."

"What does that mean?" He thought, but did not ask.

Chapter Eight

"Father, have you ever heard the story about a white deer that was followed by two riders, blood brothers who finally separated? One went back east where he came from and the other went south. 'This is my land,' he shouted. The grass was unbelievably green and juicy. The rivers were clear and the water was sweet. The sky smiled, never was there a cloud in the sky . . ." Mr. Gottlieb interrupted his son, "Yes son. I have heard that story."

He was a strong man, broad shouldered with a neck of steel. His eyes were blue. He looked like Hans Albers, the actor.

They both sat at the table, which was covered with a white cloth, plates were waiting for the steaming white potatoes that filled bowl quite modestly in the middle of the table. Wolfgang was hungry. His sister was out to the grocery store. Miraculously, eggs were available today. People called it a miracle; eggs were not available for weeks. Wolfgang's sister left a few hours ago. In those days waiting in longer lines in front of the stores for a few hours was not out of the ordinary.

It was Mr. Gottlieb who cooked the potatoes and set the table. His son's arrival called for a special meal. They only had potatoes in the house.

"It is a Hungarian saga that is concerned with the establishment of the Hungarian state around the year 900 or so. The two brothers were Ugor and Magor. Magor was the one that stayed and led his people to the land of plenty, the present Hungary. Whatever happened to Ugor remains in the clouds of folk lore."

He checked the potatoes.

"They are getting cold," he said. "Where did you hear that story?"

"I don't know. I never really heard it. I told it."

"You told it?"

"Yes, in the hospital in Passau. I was unconscious, so they said. I must have had fever and I talked. The doctors told me about it later."

The older Gottlieb gazed toward the door as if he expected his daughter to enter at any moment. Then, he turned to his son and said, "Sometimes the mind knows more than what we are willing to admit. As a matter of fact we consistently close our eyes to the work of our minds. We pay too much attention to the words that leave our lips. We don't listen to the words that talk to us deep inside because we prefer to be deaf. That keeps us comfortable."

He looked at the door again, this time anxiously. Wolfgang noticed it. What he just heard sounded confusing.

"You said, father, that I could have known this story even though I never heard it. You think that as I was moving across Hungary I could have unconsciously picked up the story because it was alive in the mind of the population?"

". . . And in the unconscious mind of those that were in the Hungarian plains," Mr. Gottlieb added.

The door opened and Giselle Gottlieb entered.

"Wolfgang," she cried, her eyes filled with tears and glistened with happiness. She hugged and kissed him.

"Women always cry when they are happy," Mr. Gottlieb said. "Quit this tear shedding, let's everybody be gay, Wolfgang is home."

***

Doctor Nándor and Mrs. Magyar rode across the undescriptive landscape. They talked about their experiences in the immediate past. She explained how the Lager was established and how one more person could be accommodated. Nothing was said about Marika.

All along the road farmers started to greet the spring. They had a way of welcoming spring. It was an emotional experience. They looked up to the sky like a son looks up to a father. More than that, they looked at the soil of their land with a hungry appetite. They listened to the message coming from every pore of the earth.

The Bavarian spring was not really alive yet even though the calendar announced its resurrection a few days earlier. Farmers were busy spreading the accumulated contents of the outhouses over their small pieces of land. They returned to the earth what they took out of it earlier. Hundreds of pieces of toilet paper and newspaper fragments littered the fields where vegetables were to grow later on.

The doctor could hardly believe his eyes. Here, in Bavaria, here where the National Socialist movement really originated, plain human excreta was used to enrich the soil. Were there no health codes in place, he wondered. The fantastic glitter of Hitler's Party rallies and later the national celebrations were in contrast to the picture of small land owners wading in human excreta and spreading it across their fields.

A few weeks later he witnessed another thing that surprised him even more. By then he did not live in the Lager any more. By then his warm feeling for Marika had cooled off. He still loved her, but it did not have the quality of "forever." His love was silent, and then communications between them were disappearing.

He moved out of the large storeroom, which the refugees called Lager, but they really meant camp. Basically they "camped" in a store room. The conditions were crowded to say the least.

Many things in the minds of many people took on different meaning in those days. They changed from day to day, from hour to hour. Religion, politics, business thinking, expectations for the future would change rapidly depending on the situation of the time. Principles were dormant for a while. There was only one thing of importance that everybody endorsed without exception—get away from the Russians.

He lived in a farmhouse now. He had a small room in a large chalet like a two story house. The room was just large enough to get out of the bed without getting out of the room. The door was to the right of the bed and opened to the hallway. The toilet, which was not a bathroom, was located next door. There was a little space at the foot of the bed for his belongings, and a little more space on the window sill to the left of the bed.

It was still cold, although the sun climbed into the April path. The house was largely unheated. Each room had a stove, an iron, and some Kachel, except his. His room, originally, must have been a closet, but if a Hungarian refugee was crazy enough to pay for a bed in the closet, so be it. It was alright with the Bavarian farmer. He demonstrated international friendship.

The toilet next door protruded from the building like a balcony. The floor space was small, accommodated only a seat that was nothing but an unpainted box anchored to the floor. There was a large circular hole in the middle and another in the floor matching the upper one. The wind and the snow riding the wind found its way up and through there. This "construction" invited a draft that found its way into the small niche. To try to urinate against the draft or to have a bowel movement became a major undertaking. Urine and feces fell freely just following gravity, but winds, and storms interfered, and splashed the secretions all over the wall of the house. When they reached the ground, they accumulated and froze into a cone in the winter. By the spring the cone had reached six feet. The life size cone of frozen shit and piss, along with the concept of *Herrenrasse,* described the condition of Germany in 1945.

One morning, as he left the house and his eyes jumped from dew drops to dew drops glistening on the few blades of grass, he saw lots of blood on the ground, probably as much as a gallon. Two men were busy dipping their hands in some of the blood that was collected in a bucket. The blood gushed from the neck of a bull with large, beautiful eyes. A large hole was cut into the left side of the neck. Through it a large rope was introduced presumably, behind a blood vessel, to regulate the bleeding that was caused by an aptly done incision. Tightening or relaxing the rope could control the rate of bleeding. One man was the landlord. The bull was his. The other man was an expert in animal disease. Not a veterinarian, just an expert. They both reached into the steaming steam of blood with their fingers, and every few seconds they pronounced their judgments. "It is not quite as sour now," the expert said while contemplating his bloodstained fingers.

The blood became less and less sour as a little time went by. The bucket got fuller, and the animal grew more and more patient and calm. Finally, the decision was made to stop the procedure because now the blood was sweet enough as determined by the expert fingers. By then the stream of blood was considerably weaker, and it did not stream as much. Maybe the weather turned a little warmer. Maybe the bull cooled off. The bleeding was stopped with some difficulty, and the bull was slowly led back to the stable. In technical terms what the doctor saw amounted to blood letting. It was the same thing that prevailed throughout the war and now was about ready to stop. According to some, the wholesale blood letting of the war was not for the sake of killing, but for cure, to cure the sour aspect of life.

Achieving cure by blood letting is as old as humanity. Now, in a vague sense Doctor Nándor started to understand why the German majority supported Hitler, at least at the beginning. In spite of modern technical advances and scientific achievements, many people lived in antiquity. Killing and blood was part of their ancestors' lives, and will take hundreds of years without wars and without letting even a drop of blood fall upon our soil before our children will be safe. The earth did not need more blood.

***

When Mrs. Magyar and the doctor reached the so called Lager, a lengthy introduction took place. During its course those who occupied the huge school store room fired literally thousands of questions at János. Real communications with the outside world were maintained through German newspapers, particularly the "*Völkischer Beobachte,*" and through the radio that continued its reporting in a monotonous fashion on a glorious end of the war and on the coming of total German victory. Some people believed what they heard and read. Others, like

Doctor Nándor just wanted to get west before an iron curtain could be erected west of their location.

The tone of the radio broadcasts started to raise superstitions. In the last few months when Hungary was under a strict dictatorship, there was much more freedom of reporting than in Germany. Even those people who readily accepted the Hungarian variation of totalitarian government disliked the monotony and clear deceitfulness of the German broadcasts. Monotony was not acceptable to Hungarians whose history, landscape, and way of life provided them with almost infinite variety.

"How did the occupying Russians behave?" That was the number one question. It was on the mind of everybody. What was the fate of those friends and relatives who were unable to or didn't want to move west?

The answer to that question was based on information that refugees brought with them, those refugees who were able to receive news from friends who were exposed to horrible indignations, human degradations, rapes, and murders. The Russians in Hungary acted like a marauding horde. Each soldier received a ration of about four ounces of vodka daily and twice that amount under fighting conditions. That answer was a powerful justification for becoming refugees, leaving their homes, their lands, and their future. A new future was waiting.

The Lager's population consisted of some thirty-five people made up by ten families. There were no partitions in the huge room. The beds were made of unpolished pine wood, produced by a local *Schreiner* carpenter, or cabinet maker. The mattresses were sacks of straw. Gray military blankets served as covers and bedspreads, and they provided warmth in the unheated room. The beds were lined up along the wall some were located in the middle next to a huge table with benches. A large brick oven occupied one corner and remained silent for lack of fuel.

The life in the Lager adjusted itself to the appearance of the room. No decoration, no adornment, no privacy. That aspect bore down on everybody's spirit. To be seen and to be heard every minute of the day pleased dictators only. It drove ordinary people insane.

Many people longed to be insane. Not really, they just needed to be different. In peace time they can afford it, but in war insanity is intolerable. The 35 Hungarians felt each other's tension, and discomfort even though, on the surface, got along beautifully. Their life resembled that of married couples whose lives are dominated by the all important appearance to the point that appearance becomes a purpose. Such a marriage, though not exactly sane, can turn out to be functional.

The refugees seemed to be happy on the surface. They cooperated with each other and operated a huge household. It was a collective undertaking. Everyday a different family took care of the cooking and cleaning. There was nothing else to do, but remember and dream. The Hungarians dream differently, so do the Germans, so do the Russians, the English, the French, and the Americans. Members of small nations dream more colorful dreams. Those who have strength on their side have drier, meatier dreams.

The Hungarian dream was scattered in the spring of 1945 all over European Asia. On the slopes of the Urals, on the banks of the Seine, they dreamed of peace, dignity, and pride. None of that would come true, not now.

The Germans dreamed of victory. It was not to be materialized. The Russians were too drunk to dream. The British, the French, the Americans were too tired. Only the losers could or were free to dream. They were free to do only that.

***

Some of the families had been in the Lager for months. They left Hungary sometime in the winter. These were families with considerable influence, and strong right wing feelings. Graft was always a part of the Hungarian scène. Money, in Hungary, had a great deal of power. Rumor said that it was not at the level that ruled in Rumania, but it was important enough. Shortly before and immediately after the so-called abdication of Horthy, the Regent, the picture started to swing away from money. It was said that Horthy was hauled away by the Germans inside a large roll of carpeting. That, of course, did not explain what happened to his wife. Nobody really knew reliable details. At that time money wasn't worth much. So influences were peddled on the basis of ideology. That meant that a large number of the population changed their colors to green in order to please the Party in power after Horthy, the Nyilas Party. It took over the functions of the government. Szálasi, the Party leader could not understand why Hitler did not put him in power earlier. Horthy could have been whisked out months earlier. In the matter of Szálasi, Hitler was wise in postponing his actual support until the very end, when the romantic incompetence of the Nyilas Party could do very little damage. People seeking favors from the National Socialistic government tried to prove their long standing loyalty or at least their anti-Semitic feelings. This way they could count on special treatment. As a result, arrangements were made with the Germans to transport to Germany along with their valuables and in fair comfort, many families who did not want to face Russian occupation. About half of the people in the Lager were in that favored position.

The others, the "ordinary people" joined later as they made their own way to the west. The Magyars were the last ones until the recent arrival of Doctor Nándor.

He was given a spot where he could put his bed as soon as he had one. He had to contact the *Schreiner* first. In the meantime, a blanket on the floor would do.

Aside from having been asked many, many times about many, many things, he was given all kinds of advice.

Generally speaking, the less people knew the more advice they gave. The doctor listened, stored and screened all that he heard, and discarded most of it later on. Most of the advice was intended to be practical and was not on truth but on sentiment. It was based on an imaginary premise, but terribly real for some, that the Hungarians were much better people than the Bavarians. They thought themselves as more intelligent, more cultured, and more urban and more everything else. Consequently the Bavarians were considered belonging to a lower mental category and therefore to be feared. The doctor was urged to be on the alert and protect himself against the homegrown stupidity. The premise that the intelligent ones should fear the stupid ones did not sit well with the doctor. A few days later when he got acquainted with some of the farmers, he found that they were hardly different from their Hungarian counter parts. They looked at their soil more commercially, were more advanced in their business thinking, and aside from their ancient fertilizing habits they were a little more productive and owned more equipment. That was true for the small farmers. There weren't any large farms in this area. Machinery kept them from sweating. With the disappearance of sweat, feelings toward soil became less personal. It made little difference to the soil.

It was late afternoon on the day when he saw Marika boarding the train; finally she had returned. Mrs. Magyar drove her fancy carriage to Pfarrkirchen to the rail station. Baron Magyar went along to have some fresh air, and they asked the doctor to ride along for "old time's sake." The "old times" were only a few weeks. Events cluttered up the hours and minutes, weeks became large and long particularly in the memory. They became "old times" that were hated by revolutionaries, treasured by romantics, and old people. People drank to "old times," and did many things for "old time's sake."

Anything done for that purpose irritated the doctor. The Magyars did not say, "Come along, surprise Marika." They said, "Come along for old time's sake."

It was almost dark when the train rolled in, and in a few minutes Marika sat next to him in the back of the carriage. It was dark by the time they arrived at the Lager.

They spoke very little that evening. It seemed as if the presence of all of the people in the room had a paralyzing effect on their vocal cords, and upon their emotional transmission into words. Marika was more affected than János. She was silent and seemed uncomfortable. After the first impetuous desire to kiss her and tell her how happy he was to see her, his emotions dropped into a cold nothingness brought about by her more than reserved attitude.

He slept on the floor. He was exhausted. In a way it felt as if he came home, not exactly a home that he felt and treasured inside along with a dream, but the kind of home that offered limited comfort, and provided a more or less permanent shelter. A room shared with other people can turn into a home. This large room was shared by many. Most of the occupants felt like the doctor. In a way, they were at home.

***

"During the war we were free to die. Soon we will be free to live," Mr. Gottlieb said and looked out of the basement window with an expression of a blind man. The small window allowed him to see very little. He looked inside and shivered.

"We did not die, father, but will we live?"

"It will depend upon what you call life, son," the elder Gottlieb answered.

The ground was shaking and rumbled deeply. Grinding machinery noise lifted dust and packed it into gray lumps. Tanks with red stars moved around with pride. The litter was monumental. Steel, plaster, stone, and brick made an almost homogenous mass that covered Berlin. Some walls did not enclose, or support anything; some daring chimneys, and a few lucky buildings stuck their heads above the debris. Almost everything was reduced to ground level and even below.

"As I see these tanks, I do not feel like fighting," Wolfgang said.

"You have nothing to fight with."

"You do not need much to fight with. We can fight with our fists if we really want to do it, but somehow I don't feel like it. We Germans need only a will to fight. My will is gone, father.

You need more than will; you need a reason. That is what you really lack. This is what we have lacked during these war years, and I wonder what reasons we will have in the future. Will we be allowed to have our own reasons? We need purpose."

"What's their purpose?" Wolfgang asked pointing to the Russians who now appeared in large numbers.

Explosion after explosion shook the basement. The Russians were jumping, running, hiding behind dirt and stone. Explosives landed, and gunfire could be heard, but there was very little organized resistance.

"Take off your uniform, son." Wolfgang did. Giselle sat in the corner crying. A little while later the Russian soldiers entered their basement. They wanted food and drink, but the Gottliebs did not have anything to give them. Then they took their watches, their rings, and looked in their mouths for gold teeth.

"You saw their purpose," the elder Gottlieb said after they left.

Day after day others came. It seemed that there was no end to the wave of unkempt dirty soldiers from the east.

"You are free now, Germans," one of them said. Later on many others said the same thing.

***

The next morning the doctor awakened refreshed. His back did not ache. His joints felt springy and relaxed. He slept on the floor on and under a blanket. He expected to be stiff, but he was not. "It is not where you sleep, but how you sleep," he thought. He had no dreams. He probably did not even turn. The night seemed short. The morning came almost immediately after he fell asleep. He woke up somewhat startled, foggy a little, mostly because temporarily he'd lost his time orientation. With opened eyes he slept a few more minutes. Then slowly, like coming from a great distance, ten o'clock in the evening entered his mind. That was when he went to bed, and he must have fallen asleep immediately.

When his eyes cleared, and the fog was gone, his brain became spongy again. That took a few minutes. He looked around for Marika. He was embarrassed when he saw her dressed. She was sitting at the table preparing batter in a large dish. He thought that maybe he was the last person to wake up. He noticed that many people were dressed, but others just were getting up. The ones dressed presented a pitiful sight. Men and women were sitting on the edge of their beds or were standing around in anticipation of nothing. Those who had just woken up acted as if everybody else was a part of a large family. They moved around in pajamas and night gowns without embarrassment. The doctor had never been in a situation that required him to appear in pajamas in front of strange people. After taking a deep breath, he crawled from under his blanket. He felt that everybody was watching him. In a way everybody was. He was the newest member of this large family. He simply had to adjust. He had to get rid of his desire for privacy.

He smiled at Marika self consciously. He needed a shave. His hair was stringy and oily. The dust of his travel found its way to the root of each hair.

One corner of the room featured a makeshift curtain. Behind it functions like bathing, washing, and personal hygiene were exercised with all of their accompanying sounds.

He took his razor from his bundle. With the help of crude soap manufactured right in the Lager from pieces of fat and lye that were left at mealtime he did a decent job shaving. The same soap washed his hair and made him feel reasonably well. A piece of soap can do that. It can make you feel well when nothing else can.

He smiled at Marika again and sat down next to her on the bench.

"Breakfast? We're having pancakes this morning," she pointed to the batter.

"How is cooking organized?"

"Everyday a different family takes turn. You've been attached to our family; you will have to help with cooking today."

He got to the Lager just yesterday. He wondered who attached him to the Magyar family in such a hurry, but he did not ask.

"It will be great. What's my assignment?"

"First is first. Get dressed first."

"Of course."

He felt embarrassed. He started to look for some clean clothes in his bundle. Strangely his thoughts were concentrated on the batter, not Marika. He wondered where the flour for the batter came from. Later after breakfast he was told to see the Bürgermeister to receive his *Lebensmittelm Karte*, his food rations. The Bavarian government provided the Hungarian refugees with the same food rations as the general population.

"You will have to unpack today and take an inventory; all have taken inventories. That way nothing gets lost in the wash."

"Is washing a community affair too?" he asked.

"More or less. Of course, nicer pieces cannot be boiled on the stove, but in general we throw everything into one large pot. See that one?"

A huge galvanized pot with a wooden lid steamed on the hot plate of the wood burning stove.

"Your assignment is to gather wood. There are forests all around us. It is easy. The mayor of the town allows us to gather wood, provided we do not cut anything down. We are just to pick up the branches pitched there by the elements. The branches literally smother the ground."

"It will be great, Marika." He looked at her and continued. "When I was a kid and wandered in the woods of the Mecsek Mountains, I frequently picked up the branches to see what was under them. I was curious, and it was fascinating. I never thought that the fascination of picking up branches would turn into a purposeful activity. It still can be fascinating."

"When do I start?" He asked smiling. He realized immediately that what he asked was a sign of submission, or at least could be construed as such, but he did not care. She was there, and he was near her. He had the same impression of her now as he did when they first met. She was a terrific sum of her various parts, an end product much better than expected from just looking at her face, arms, body, legs, skin. She was harmony alive. Not harmony of a well created sculpture, but that of life. She was a hard person to describe, not really beautiful, but terribly attractive.

She was warm, but not close. She spoke with him with strange reservations. The voice had not changed. It was her eyes that made János feel that she was surrounded by cool air, not cold, just uncomfortable. Back in Szombathely she had been warm, uninhibited, and natural. Not now.

Marika was right. Dry branches from the storms of previous years covered the ground holding back the weak blades of grass that just started to come alive. The Bavarian spring was late. There was no evidence of violets that carpeted the Hungarian landscape to make the flow of blood more glamorous. Here a few daffodils peeped around to see if they could trust the first waves of warm breeze. Nature was distrustful; it still had the memory of a cold winter. The soil still shivered a little. There were many large branches that the doctor piled up neatly as if to put an order into nature's way of things.

Years make their mark. We see them everywhere. They are in our faces. We see them in our cemeteries; our history is a collection of the marks produced by years. The dead, dry branches are scattered for the future to decay and to burn to ashes just as the war is turning to decay and fire. "Just like the war," he heard himself talking.

"Give me the years of the future to see," he shouted.

"What is the matter, János?" Marika was standing and watching him.

Her voice was sweet almost like in Szombathely. He moved towards her.

"Nothing, nothing," he said. "Just give me the years to see. I want to see your years and mine. I want to see the future, Marika."

Now, he stood next to her. His arms moved spontaneously around her and he held her. Her arms were crossed on her chest. They were a barrier. Her lips were cold and detached from her, almost like floating. He tried to press his lips against hers, but they felt distant, not approachable. He felt uneasy, let down. His arms dropped. His shoulders sagged as though coming down from a shrug. He felt heavy, very heavy.

***

There was a noise a little to the left. It was a crackling noise as if someone was walking on the dry branches. János and Marika stood still. They heard a groaning noise and what appeared be heavy breathing. A man in a striped prison attire, haggard, unshaven with short irregularly cut hair staggered into the small clearing. His large shoes led the way. He followed them unsteadily. He looked at them with expressionless eyes. Suddenly he fell on one knee and tried to tie his shoelace. He could not get up. Now, his eyes came alive a little; a small flicker was noticeable in them. He spoke and said in German, "Please help me."

The doctor rushed to his side. With a little help from the doctor, he got up. He did not say thank you. He was very unsteady. The doctor kept supporting him.

"The Americans will be here soon," the man said. He had a foreign accent.

"Are you an escaped prisoner?" The doctor asked.

"No, Kazettler."

"How do you know about the Americans?"

"They will be here," the man answered. "They are in Arnsdorf."

Arnsdorf was not very far. If the Americans were really in Arnsdorf, it would take only a day or less to get here. In reality it took two weeks. The Americans were not in Arnsdorf. They were there in the hoping mind of that man. The Americans were his only hope.

In a few words he explained that he escaped from a concentration camp and had spent the last two weeks in the woods. He was heading west to reach the Americans faster. He could not wait for them to come. He represented the feelings of millions of people from Eastern Europe.

"You are not strong enough to continue," the doctor said.

"I don't need much strength; they will be here soon." With that he continued his journey across the branches adding manmade sound to the voice of spring. It resulted in disharmony.

The doctor felt a sense of depression overtake him. Frustration in his personal life came at the same time as his frustration with the world. He looked long upward not really seeing anything, but asking the question, "What now?"

It was for the first time, now in April of 1945 that he heard the expression *Kazettler*. That expression could be heard all across Germany over and over, perhaps a million times, after the war. It was really the first time that he had a concept of what a concentration camp was. He could not recall an episode where any discussion centered around concentration camps. Either he alone was blind, or a whole segment of population was blind. He must have been a member of that segment. He knew from psychology and psychiatry that unpleasant situations can be blocked out of the memory. He wondered if that may have happened to him.

Had he known about the concentration camps, would he be here now? The answer was yes. He did not come to Germany to hate the Germans. He had begun his journey to get far enough west to avoid the Russians, and to experience the Americans. To go west he had to go to Germany. The sun must follow a path; a refugee must take a certain road. That's what he did.

He asked Marika whether she knew about the concentration camps, and if she had known about them, what she would have done. The answer was similar to his, identical really.

***

There was an obvious change in Marika. She was not the same person he met in Szombathely. She was not the same person he saw for the first time when the episode of the louse occurred. She was not the same woman he kissed when they took their risky journey to salvage much needed medicine. He wanted to ask her about her love for him, but he let the question die before it reached his lips. He tied the branches together with a rope and carried them on his right shoulder as they walked back to the Lager. They walked in a light, careless fashion. One would have thought they were singing. But there were no sounds. The Bavarian landscape was somber. When they walked for the medical supply, the sky and the air and the fields were smiling. Not because they were part of Hungary, but because they knew that János and Marika were in love. The Bavarian landscape read their emotions and noticed a difference.

For a short time, just a few seconds, he blamed himself. Maybe he had changed. Maybe she was the same and he was different. The self blame did not last long. It was Marika who had changed.

When they got back to the Lager, they found it in an uproar. It was restless. It looked as if it had its own life independent of the many individuals. A multitude of people in time came alive as if they were one unit, demonstrating, and revolting; foolish games resulted a time when individuals united for a purpose or no purpose at all. Then the individual disappears and the crowd lives an individual life.

"The Russians are coming," was the greeting that met the doctor and Marika at the door.

It sounded improbable to the doctor that the Russians would be anywhere near. Some radio stations in Slovakia were still on the air many miles to the east. He knew that blood was cheap in the suburbs of Berlin. He knew that hearts were beating fast along the eastern front, but he could not believe that the front would be so near. He did not feel it in his own heart.

The panic in the Lager was real. It was, of course, not based on anything official or reliable. Panics are based seldom on something official or even tangible. They are based on anxiety and fear. Fear has a way of creeping around blood vessels. It can hide there for a long time, until it suddenly reaches the heart. Then fear was discovered. Temples throbbed, pupils dilated, and fingers trembled. Fear had its triumph. That was the mechanism of panic that swept over everybody.

Something had to be done, some kind of action, what kind nobody knew. There was great commotion. The agitation was generalized. The doctor had a hard time finding out just what was going on. Finally, somebody explained to him that a few German soldiers, coming from the east, had moved across the village and claimed that the Russians were close behind.

To the doctor the whole thing sounded unreasonable. There was very little that he could do to influence the unruly crowd.

Three men were arguing at a table. They were quite loud. One was pounding on a large enameled can, making the lid jump up and down creating a rattling noise. It was a lard can with small pinpoint openings in the lid for ventilation holes, large enough for air, small enough for keeping insects out. Now the enamel was shattered; little chips were scattered on the floor.

The argument arose out of the perceived need to salvage at a time when it would become necessary for the entire Lager to move west to flee the Russians.

The point in question was lard. In peace time lard was an important element in the Hungarian kitchen. Lack of it could mean disaster. Many Hungarians grew up on bread and lard and as babies on pap made of flour and lard. In the spring of 1945 lard was more important to many Hungarians than milk.

It was not surprising that many held an emotional attachment to the food that nourished them, that gave them strength through the years. In war time, whatever attachment an individual had became exaggerated, and virtually ritualized. In the Lager the possession of lard was an all important ritual

Each family had a large can where they kept the all important lard. The cans resembled huge coffee pots and had a capacity up to 40 pounds. Each morning the lady of the family who was responsible for the good condition of their possession and also their economic welfare inspected the lard can to make sure that the night did not deplete this valuable food. Had the pigs known how highly their fat was esteemed, they would have died happier and with much less squealing.

Now, that there was again a Russian threat in the middle of Bavaria, someone conceived the idea that the lard should be divided evenly so that every person would have the same amount to carry. Moving farther west was not even debated; it was a given fact. As with ideas in general, good or bad, there was quite a bit of trouble. First of all, an inventory had to be taken and the exact amount on hand had to be determined. Then the weight of the lard had to be divided by the number of people. At that point, things went fairly smoothly.

Then the lard had to be divided. Then the pounding began.

Marika and the doctor awoke at this crucial moment.

While three men argued putting years of reputation behind each word, some of the ladies placed a pair of scales on the table and took up position silently near the three nervous men. The ladies' presence calmed the emotions of the men. The can lid was lifted soon, and the lard was weighed kilo after kilo. Each unit went to a different person. When the round was completed, it started all over again. When one can was empty, the next one followed. Eventually the lard was evenly divided. As a result some were richer, some were poorer, but peace had prevailed.

Of course the Russians never came. Nobody was disappointed in spite of the drastic steps taken to salvage the lard.

***

The Lager in the store room of the school house was located along the highway that cut the village into northern and southern segments. It was built on a hill overlooking the entire village with its loosely connected yards and one whitewashed church. As one looked out of the large window to the south one could see the house, and the shop of the *Schreiner* (carpenter). Everybody just referred to him as *Schreiner.* Nobody used his last name nor his first name.

There are people who remain nameless all of their lives. Others exist only in their nick names, which are like no names at all. In the case of the *Schreiner* there was a particular situation where the Hungarians were not aware. In general, the Hungarians were aware of very little except the whereabouts of the Russians. They really did not know anything about that. They more or less guessed, and jittered, or relaxed accordingly. What they definitely did not know was that to be called a *Schreiner* was an honor status as much as that of the *Bürgermeister* or of the *Lehrer.* In ancient Germany craftsmen and professionals were respected and valued. That tradition reached into 1945. To be called *Schreiner* and not Herr so and so seemed funny for the Hungarians. A lot of contrast was noted by everybody. This was just one example.

To the east there was an open field of green pasture, which shimmered in the early rays in the sun. Later it was timid green. To the south a few houses adorned a small hill. It was called Kammerhut. After the American occupation, the doctor moved there into his small, closet like room.

About a mile or so to the east the highway ran into a larger road leading to Pfarrkirchen. The doctor walked to Pfarrkirchen many times in the months to come. It was on this road that he met an American soldier who spoke Hungarian. "It won't be long and you will be able to go home," he said.

The doctor realized then that most American soldiers had no idea about the world of the refugees. Specifically, they were not informed about the atrocious behavior of the Russian Army. That many Hungarians had no intentions of returning to their homeland had not entered their minds. The American Armed Forces Radio Network paid no attention to the refugees, not then. A war had to be concluded, and peace had to be organized, prisoners of war had to be handled; there was much to do.

Everywhere in the picturesque valley Hungarian refugees populated schoolhouses, barns, and abandoned buildings. Many lived with Bavarian families. The impact of strangers with their strange thinking and strange culture made an impression upon the population. This impression was a combination of fear and admiration. Little by little the two cultures lived in symbiosis. When the war was over, the inventiveness of the Hungarians along with their skill and courage to defy authority made them a valuable ally.

One day in April the air was heavy and restless. Some people with good ears and sensitive hearts began to hear machine gun fire. For a few hours blood vessels tightened, and there was quiet again. There was a feeling of profound tiredness, and a massive let down. Letting the past go was hard; the future was slow to materialize.

The next morning, only a few minutes after breakfast when the dishes were still piled up unwashed, there was a strange timid knock on the door. One does not have to be an expert; one has to be alive a little to understand the quality of the knocking. If one lives in a Lager, one develops a sense of alertness for noise and everything else that is able to manifest itself. The knock was quiet, hardly noticeable. Yet it had the power to stop the vocal cord, paralyze the diaphragm, and create silence.

"*Herein,*" come in somebody said.

The door opened slightly, then the door opened all the way, and the Bürgermeister of Peterskirchen II along with five other men stood in the doorway. They looked pale and panic stricken. Their faces were tense. They were ushered into the room by the refugees who breathed with relief. One always breathes easier when the danger is past. Why they suspected danger in the first place, they really could not explain.

The Bavarians acted as if they had just come over for a little chat and commented how neat the Lager looked. This was acknowledged with thanks and with anticipation of what really brought their visitors early in the morning.

"Did you hear the machine guns yesterday?" The Bürgermeister asked finally.

"See I did not hallucinate." Mrs. Magyar snapped at her husband.

"Mother," whispered Marika.

"Yes," they heard it. Most of them did.

"The Americans will be here soon," the Bürgermeister continued. "This is a nice little town," he added.

It was nice, indeed, but actually, what was he after? There was an oppressing silence. Nobody moved.

"It would be awful to see it destroyed."

The Hungarians searched for each other's glances. They were questioning. What was this all about? They waited. The silence got heavier. Finally, the Bürgermeister, after receiving encouraging nods from the others asked in a voice that lacked volume and was more squeezed than spoken, "Are you going to fight?"

At that point the Lager came alive with sounds of deep breaths and joys of surprise. The facial expressions communicated even more. Then there was silence again like in a courtroom when the accused admits his crime. Suddenly the Lager was exhausted.

The doctor recovered first. He stood up and in fairly good German he explained to the visitors what the spontaneous outburst of sighs and shouts indicated. That they knew that the situation was delicate and critical and that the Hungarians only wanted to be free. They did not want to fight. His speech was risky, he knew that. If the Bavarians' intention was to recruit them for a last ditch resistance, then they would be in trouble. The tone of the Bavarian delegation, the introductory remarks, indicated no desire to fight. He tried to speak with them and find out a little more about their intentions, but they paid no attention to him. They sat there as if delivered from all evil. Salvation sparkled in their eyes, and their heads glowed with happiness. They looked like friends. Their smiles were endless.

"Thank God," the Bürgermeister said. "We were afraid that you might want to fight."

With that the war came to an end in Peterskirchen II. The occupation took place a few days later. In many communities the war ended in the same fashion on the western front. It ended with a will to live, with a commitment for life.

***

During the weeks that the doctor stayed in the Lager, Marika made frequent trips to Passau, to Eggenfelden, and to other places that she did not mention to him. He still remembered Szombathely and was still hanging on to her as she was then. He hoped that she would return to her previous self.

She said that times had changed rapidly and that she had to keep up with them. She urged János to do the same, but she did not say what she meant. He started to feel uncomfortable around her, but he blamed himself for that.

At the same time an element of happiness crept into his emotions. Not the happiness of love, but an indescribable happiness of being emotionally free. Marika was at a distance now. She managed to move away from him slowly, calculatingly without hurting him in an obvious way. She smiled, but she was inaccessible. She would not discuss the past, not even the past before they had met. When he showed her the picture the Feketes gave him, she showed no emotion.

He still loved her, but his love was now in the comfort of a secret. Things that one did not mention remained subjective and could remain that way. Objectivity required declaration by some form, word, or action. He said nothing substantial to Marika. They just talked. In a way he was happy because he was free.

The activity in the air was on the increase. Everyday low flying aircraft frightened the people at first, and then the planes became a part of their daily life. The village shared the sky now. It was all right; it even felt good.

The machine gun sounded now like a percussion instrument in a symphony. To the population they spoke of life. Nobody wanted to hear a eulogy in machine gun language. For many hours the shooting remained at the same distance.

There was silence for many hours. There wasn't any traffic. Nobody ventured out into the street, not even into the back yard. The chickens scratched the softening ground unconcerned. Pigeons woke up to the mystery of spring way up in the belfry of the church. The bird's love was for the fighting world to see.

The doctor left the building and walked across the green pasture to the south. He did not know why. He just wanted to reach the highway running to the north. He just wanted to see. He wanted to be the first one to visualize the occupational forces. Overhead airplanes buzzed at a nervous speed, but they paid no attention to him. He reached the highway. He stood on the pavement stiff legged, with his feet firmly anchored. On the north at a great distance a brown mass started to move. He could not see what it was.

He hurried back to the Lager.

"They are coming," he reported.

Now he felt even more free. His personal life was free now. Marika was just another lovely person whose life was separated from his. She was like flowers in a room, separated from the rest of the room, just a decoration, nothing else. He felt happy. His long journey would be rewarded soon. He stood in the large green, school building doorway, his hands were behind him to make his lungs fill with more air. His hair invited the wind. His eyes met the clouds and the silver of the sky. His skin communicated with the rivers.

On the left, a noise produced by motors asked his ears for attention. A column of American jeeps appeared at the curve maybe a mile away. It approached rapidly. The first and the last vehicles of the unit had machine guns mounted in the middle.

"Only a minute and a half, only one hundred and five more beats," his heart said.

The jeeps came closer. The soldiers did not smile, but they did not express hate. One could see that. One of the soldiers pointed his pistol at the door. The doctor smiled at the barrel. The jeep slowed down and the soldier held the weapon with a steady, youthful hand. The doctor had a youthful smile. The jeep kept moving slowly to the east. The soldier kept aiming. The jeep suddenly disappeared around the curve behind the Pfarrer's house. The doctor closed his eyes. The movement of the small muscles in his eyelids announced exuberantly that he was free . . . .

Suddenly the streets filled with people, smiling waving at the ever increasing number of soldiers. They now smiled as the soldiers tossed candy and chewing gum into the crowd. The people waved, cheered, and almost danced.

The doctor did not feel like cheering. He went into the house to be alone. He wanted to be all alone with his freedom. He wanted to worship it, for his freedom was god-like.

About the Author

Joseph J. Kozma is a physician in private practice in Jacksonville, Illinois. His publications include *Long Distance Murder* (mystery novel), *Mathematics in Color,* (poetry), *Until We Meet* (poetry), *Killer Plants* (poisonous plant guide) and two chap books, *Of song, of Life* and *Solitary Bee.*

Kozma was born in *Pécs,* Hungary, and European Capital of Culture. He had a first hand knowledge of the plight of the Hungarian refugees in the spring of 1945. Their choice was clear, Russian occupation and years of oppression and exploitation or freedom in the west.

Books by Pearn and Associates, Inc.

Novels:
1945, Joseph J. Kozma, (fiction), paper *
Another Chance, Joe Naiman, (fiction — publisher only) cloth
Light Across the Alley, The Story of a Young Matchmaker,
   Victor W. Pearn (fiction) Kindle Books only*
Point Guard, Victor Pearn (fiction) cloth

Nonfiction:
A Lenten Journey Toward Christian Maturity, William E.
   Breslin (prayer guide) paper
Black 14: The Rise, Fall and Rebirth of Wyoming Football,
   Ryan Thorburn (sports biography) paper
Cowboy Up: Kenny Sailors, The Jump Shot and Wyoming's Championship Basketball History,
   Ryan Thorburn, (sports biography) paper
Dream Season, My Brother Gary and the 1957 Ashland Panthers
   Victor W. Pearn (sports biography) Kindle Books only*
Goulash and Picking Pickles, Louise Hoffmann (biography) cloth
Ikaria: A Love Odyssey on a Greek Island, Anita Sullivan
   (biography) paper *
I Look Around for my Life, John Knoepfle (biography) cloth*
It Started & Ended: **The Story About a Soldier and Civilian Life**,
   Bud Grounds (biography) paper
Lost Cowboys: The Bud Daniel Story, and Wyoming Baseball,
   Ryan Thorburn (sports biography) paper
The Great Adventure—UNTOLD, Charles Hamman, (nonfiction) cloth*

Poetry:
Mathematics in Color, Joseph J. Kozma (poetry) paper
The Dreamer and the Dream, Rick E. Roberts (poetry) paper
Until We Meet, Joseph J. Kozma (poetry) paper
Walking in Snow, John Knoepfle (poetry) paper

Available on Barnesandnoble.com, Amazon.com, (also available from Ingram Books, and Baker and Taylor) you may order at your local bookstore or directly from the publisher, Pearn and Associates, Inc.
happypoet@hotmail.com. 970-599-8924   *Available on Kindle Books.

CPSIA information can be obtained at www.ICGtesting.com
Printed in the USA
243733LV00006B/1/P